Praise for

Cancer, Faith & Butterflies

"a process of metamorphosis, a journey of divine transformation. It depicts the ugliness of a hardened heart, bereft in despair, transformed into a soaring, beautiful soul. This story causes you to get in touch with your own mortality; it challenges you to discover what really is important in life. "It is not up to us to understand His plan; it's just about having faith" - this statement is the theme of this heart wrenching story. Whether it is the lack or abundance of faith is the fabric that holds this story together. Sanchez's writing style is unhurried; it is very patient. He delicately interweaves his cast of characters, causing their paths to cross, stitching them together with precision.

The story is told from the point of view of Joey. His thoughts, actions and emotions are prevalent as the narrative unfolds. Joey faces possibly the greatest conflict man can face - man versus God. Yes, his character endures loss and betrayal, but his genuine battle is understanding God.

The cast of supporting characters is essential to the narrative. They bring a touch of innocence, a voice of reason, abiding strength and grace within the storm of hopelessness, and prove that even wayfaring strangers can be secret messengers from God. Cancer, Faith and Butterflies reveals the lengths, heights and depths that God will perform to prove His great love for us. There is no place we can hide when God pursues us. We can cocoon ourselves in hardened shells, but through God's grace, He transforms us into lovely butterflies of His Providence." -- - **Cheryl E. Rodriguez, Author of** *"What's Your Story* **&** *Exposed"*

"a captivating story about love and faith that will tug at your heartstrings. It is the tale of a man's pain that seemed to have no end and how it made him question his faith. Joe's pain and suffering has many vital lessons for the reader about finding the best in life, losing it all, hitting rock bottom in your faith, and finding yourself again. It is testimony that at every moment in life, even at the most trying of times, God is always with us. Johnny M. Sanchez captures precious moments and raw emotions with his words, giving us an amazing story that will touch many hearts. This is a story about love, pain, loss, miracles, and divine enlightenment. Thank you, Johnny M. Sanchez, for one of the most amazing, most profound and most memorable stories I have ever read. You might want to keep some tissues handy; I had tears in my eyes the entire time I was reading this story, but I also had many smiles for the beautiful miracles that glowed through the shadows." - **Faridah Nassozi,** *"Freelance Writer & Speaker"*

"a well-written story. So human, and so believable. It's a very inspiring story. The prose is beautiful and the author has the gift of touching the deepest fears in readers and creating a stream of consciousness in characters that readers will easily identify with. This beautiful story reminded me so much of Tears at Night, Joy at Dawn: Journal of a Dying Seminarian by Andrew Robinson. It's a powerful testament of faith, featuring very normal and believable characters, asking questions that everyone faced with the mystery of suffering and faith would ask. Johnny M. Sanchez has created a beautiful and moving story that readers will want to keep in their hearts, especially during trying moments." - **Christian Sia reviewer for** *"Reader' Favorite's"*

"took me through myriad emotions as I began to look through the eyes of Johnny M. Sanchez in his character Joe. Cancer, Faith, & Butterflies was so well-written that it had a surreal element to its storyline, as if you were watching a movie. I felt like I was a part of the book. As a believer, whether it's cancer, or any other type of illness, the path we are traveling in our lessons is not always about us, but others. In all things seek Him, meditate on His word day and night. Just as for Joe, it was Brooke's unwavering walk that was the catalyst to his personal relationship with God." - **Vernita Naylor, Small Business Owner & author of "*Get the Cheese, Avoid the Traps*"**

"a very personal story to me. My own grandfather passed away from cancer this year and it seemed like author Sanchez knew exactly how I felt. He writes about the confusion and heartbreak with such detail that I instantly related to the characters, and I feel many other readers will as well. And the faith message written into this novel is touching and yet realistic. There are no magical changes of heart nor does everything instantly poof into perfection. It's a tough road, but it ends the way it should. Not only is this a great read for a rainy summer day, but I feel there are life lessons that can be gleaned from the pages and the characters within them. I hope to read more from author Sanchez, and enjoy more of the touching, realistic situations he creates. A beautiful piece with minimal errors." **Samantha Coville, Book Editor & author of "*Blood Oath & Blood Island*"**

Cancer, Faith & Butterflies

Cancer, Faith & Butterflies

HOW DO YOU BELIEVE WHEN YOUR WORLD FALLS APART?

Johnny M. Sanchez

Website - www.JohnnyMSanchez.com
Instagram - Johnny.Sanchez99
Facebook -Johnny M. Sanchez

Book Cover Art Created by Pro-Book
Certain stock imagery © Shutterstock
And such images are being used for illustrative purposes only.
Author photo provided by Melissa Estrada Photography.
Editor- Courtney Lindemann
ISBN: 0998367508

ISBN: 978-0-9983675-0-7 (paper-back)
ISBN: 978-0-9983675-1-4 (e-book)
Printed in the United States of America

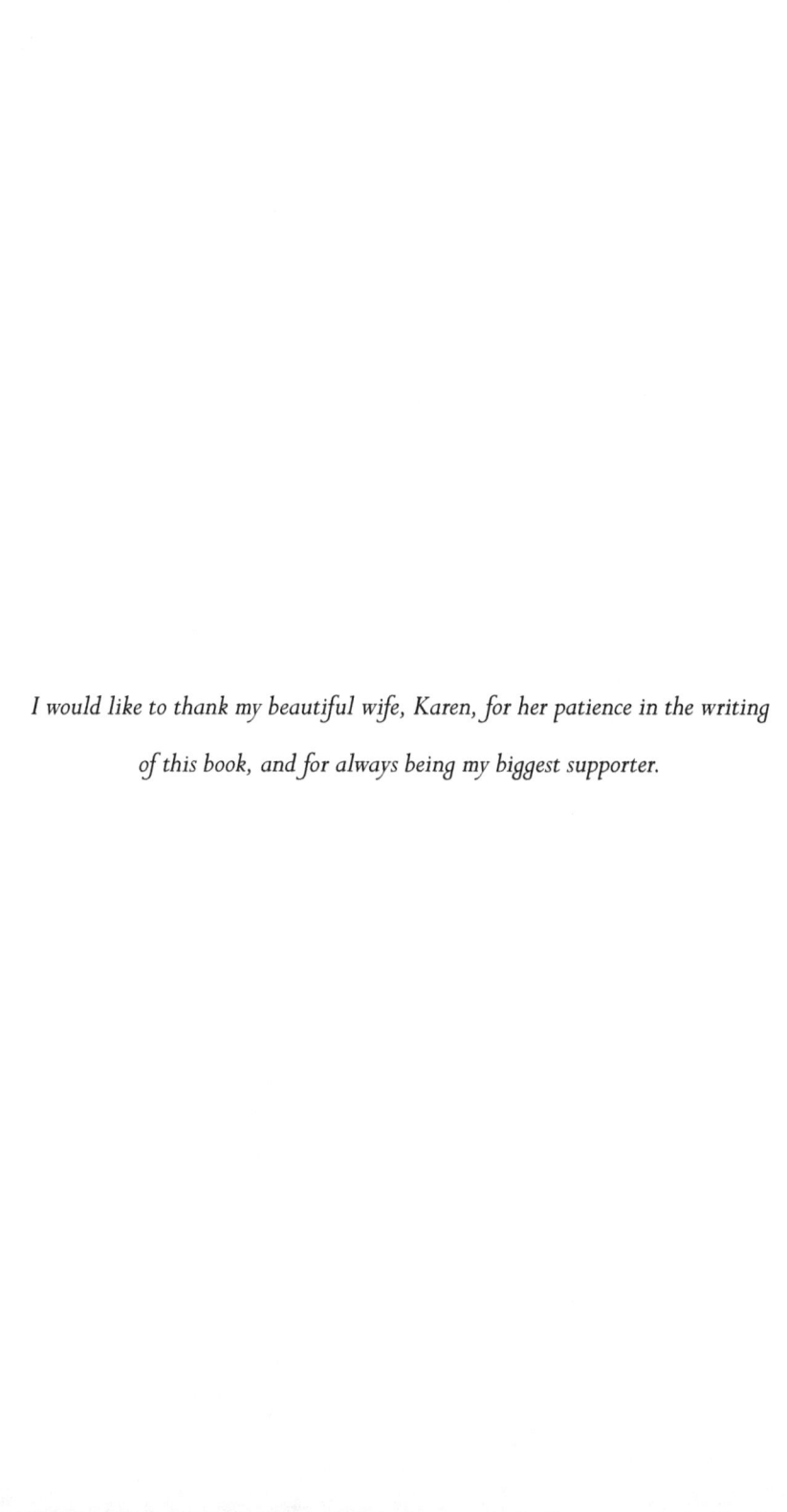

I would like to thank my beautiful wife, Karen, for her patience in the writing of this book, and for always being my biggest supporter.

This book is dedicated to:

My aunt, Lorraine Galaviz, who lost her fight with breast cancer. Love you always Tia Lola.

My cousin, Cornelio J. Lara III, who lost his fight with colon cancer. Miss You Primo Cheese.

My dear friend, Maryellen Gale Sanchez, who lost her fight with cervical cancer.

You'll be missed Nena.

My little cousin Xavier Arriaga, who did not get taken by cancer, but was taken far too soon.

Love & Miss you Primo Boo-boo.

To all who've lost their fight with cancer or who have lost a loved one.

And to those who are currently in your fight with cancer, never lose hope or faith. My mother-in-law, Juanita Carreño, is a testament to this fact. She never wavered in her hope, faith, and prayers. She was diagnosed with non-Hodgkin lymphoma cancer, stage four, in 2003. I watched as the chemo made her frail and took her hair. Even I had doubts and told my wife to prepare herself for the worst. But, my mother-in-law sat in the hospital, not once believing that cancer would beat her. She always said, "I give the glory to God, and I believe he will heal me." She beat cancer in 2004 and has been in remission ever since.

Footprints in the Sand

One night I had a dream.

I dreamed I was walking along the beach with the Lord...

Across the sky flashed scenes from my life...

For each scene, I noticed two sets of

Footprints in the sand, one belonging to me, and the other to the Lord...

When the last scene of my life flashed before me,

I looked back at the footprints in the sand.

I noticed that many times along the path of my life

There was only one set of footprints. I also noticed that it happened at

The very lowest and saddest times in my life...

This really bothered me, and I questioned the Lord about it:

"Lord, you said that once I decided to follow you, you'd walk with

me all the way. But I have noticed that during the most troublesome

times in my life there is only one set of footprints. I don't understand why

when I need you most you would leave me."

The Lord replied: "My precious child, I love you and would

Never leave you. During your times of trial and suffering, when you see

Only one set of footprints, it was then that I carried you."

By Mary Stevenson, 1939

CHAPTER 1

Jimmy

As I put the fourth quarter in the coffee machine, it made a rattling noise that sounded like it was about to give out. After six months, I'm still drinking this cheap coffee. *Damn it, of all the stinking days, now you decide to break.* I slammed my fist into the damn coffee machine. It shook roughly before sitting back in place. I put my head down, noticing the lady behind me walking away. The family sitting in the waiting room just stared at me. I didn't care; I was tired. I felt sick to my stomach, and as I looked down the dim hallway I had just come down, I dreaded walking back—seeing her lying there helpless. *Why God, why her? Six months she's been here in pain, please God I can't go through another night of seeing her like this.* My eyes watered up. I thought, *what am I doing? I'm still here at this damn machine just staring down the hall.*

I stood up straight and looked right back at the family that was still staring at me. There was an elderly woman with two young men and a little girl, who couldn't have been more than four. She was a cute little girl. They were of Asian descent; I wasn't sure if it was their custom to stare, but I wasn't in the mood, so I just stared right back. They probably thought that I broke that coffee maker. Well, little do they know, I've been fighting with that machine for the last six months. As I stared, the little girl smiled at me, and I couldn't help but think about Sara—about how she will look with the same pig-tails this little girl has when she gets to that age. I couldn't help it; I broke into a smile and nodded my head toward the little girl. She shied away and grabbed the old woman's hand.

I turned my head and stared down the hall again before I continued to walk, shaking off the throb in my hand from punching that damn coffee machine. It felt good, the pain in my hand; maybe because it helped me think about something else for a minute or two. The closer I got to the room, the less I felt the pain in my hand. I stopped right in front of the door, looked up at the plaque marking room number 409 and heard the nurses across from me laughing. There was a nursing station with two nurses on duty tonight. I overheard one of them saying that she was off at 10:30 and still had time to meet her boyfriend at this bar downtown, Titos Bar & Grill. She said, "I'm going to make the best of what's left of this Saturday."

Saturday... I thought, *I didn't even know it was Saturday.* I put my hand on the door and managed a smile as I remembered one night when Brooke and I got hammered there. She loved their guacamole and chips. I remember teasing her that she was going to turn green from eating all that guacamole. *Saturday. Damn, that means tomorrow is Sunday. I forgot to call Carroll and tell her that I'll be there at 8:00 am to pick up Sara.* I slowly pushed the door open; there she laid, quiet and peaceful. My heart dropped as I saw her flinch in pain. I ran to her side, noticing that it took all of her strength to turn and look at me. She managed a smile; I couldn't help but break into a half-hearted smile too. I knew she was in pain, but Brooke has always been a strong woman. Knowing her, she probably didn't think I could take seeing her in pain; so she held it in and made it seem like she was fine. My eyes began to water again. She just looked at me lovingly, as she always did. A tear slid down my cheek, getting caught in two weeks of facial hair that was taking on the appearance of a beard. I didn't care how I looked; I stared at her, trying not to break down completely as she slowly lifted her frail arm to wipe my cheek. Then, she slowly slid two fingers down my face, resting them on my chin, and gave me a smile as I put my two fingers on her chin and smiled. She softly rubbed her hand against the facial hair I had grown and made that face she makes when she's displeased.

One winter, we spent some time up in Montana with her grandparents, Frank and Katheryn. They are the most loving people you could ever meet. Frank had a full-on beard; he looked like he was one of the uncles on that TV show Duck Dynasty. Her cousins all had a bit of scruff too. We stayed up in Montana for five weeks; it was beautiful. I didn't shave for the first three weeks; I kind of started to like the look and wanted to try something new. Brooke completely hated it and gave me the same look she was giving me now, saying, "You can keep the beard, if I can cut my hair." She knew I would never let her cut that beautiful, dirty-blonde hair of hers. I loved the way it flowed over her shoulders. I would always come from behind, hold her by the waist, and nestle my nose in her hair. I was in Heaven. So of course, I had to shave.

As I stared at her now, even though all her hair was gone from the chemo, I looked into those deep, beautiful green eyes and thought, *she is still the most beautiful thing I've ever laid eyes on.* I took her hands from the hair on my face, brought them to my lips, and softly kissed her palms.

"I'll shave first thing in the morning," I smiled. Suddenly, she pulled her hand away quickly to cover her mouth as she began coughing profusely—her body trembled from the pain. I held her as her body jerked; it would jerk so bad that I sometimes thought it would break her back. As I held her, the last cough splattered blood through her hands and ended up on my right shoulder. I held her, praying for it to stop; these attacks were becoming more and more frequent. Finally, her body relaxed. I laid her back as gently as possible. She just laid there with her eyes closed, squinting from the pain. I tried my best not to scream to the Heavens, *why is this happening! Why her?* I took two quick steps to the sink, grabbed a towel, soaked it with warm water, rung it out, and walked back over to her. I began to clean the blood off her hands and wiped her face ever so gently. She laid very still.

I whispered, "Do you want me to change you?" She slowly nodded her head, and I began to do what I'd become accustomed to over the past months. It became like a dance we had perfected; she would slowly lift her arms, holding them straight out in front of her body, while I gently unbuttoned the top button of her nightgown from behind her neck. I lifted the gown softly, sliding it off her arms, and threw it in the basket in the corner of the room. I wet another towel with warm water and went to her, softly wiping her neck, arms, and chest. I could see the scars left from the operation. I remember how hard it was for her to come to terms with losing her breasts. They thought they had caught it in time; we were optimistic, but the lab results showed otherwise. They said it had spread to other parts of her body. Then, they started the chemotherapy. After months of testing and watching her waste away, I sometimes wondered if it would have been better to just take her home without the chemo. She seemed stronger and not really *that* sick back then. Now, after months of chemo and watching her go through the daily trauma of it—all for nothing—they stopped and said it didn't take. I remember wanting to punch the doctor in the mouth. I kept shouting at him, "It didn't take! It didn't take! You put my wife through hell for what? You said it would help, but it didn't take! YOU BAST—" I was holding Brooke's hand when he came in to tell us the status of her lab results. When she heard what I was about to say next, she squeezed my hand so I held my tongue. I just put my head down. I could see Carroll outside the door holding Sara. She started to cry as she overheard our conversation. Brooke and Carroll had become close over the years; so close that they called each other 'Sis'. I used to make jokes telling Brooke, "She's my little sister, not yours."

I continued to wipe her with the warm towel and looked at her as I cleaned. She began to relax. I sighed as I threw the towel in the basket, which was starting to fill up. I could hear those damn nurses laughing and talking. *Why don't they do their job and empty this basket?* I was about to go say something to them when I saw Brooke trembling. She was getting cold—that's another thing about this place, they always kept it so cold. *Damn this hospital!* I grabbed another gown, she slowly lifted her arms, but never opened her eyes. I smiled, thinking about this dance we've perfected. As I snapped the button behind her neck, I covered her with a blanket and kissed her forehead. I told her that I'd be right back. She nodded, and I walked out the room. I walked over to the nurses' station. One of them said, "How can we help you Mr. Connelly?" I tried not to seem upset, but I could tell they knew I wasn't in the best of moods. All of the nurses here kind of kept out of my way; you could say that I haven't exactly been the friendliest guy here. Especially that time I came back after taking care of some things, and found one of the nurses cleaning Brooke after one of her attacks. She was half off the bed, uncomfortable, and the nurse was scrubbing and jabbing at the blood on her arm. I stormed in, walked straight to the nurse, yanked the towel out of her hand, and told her, "What the hell are you doing?"

She calmly responded, "Well, cleaning your wife, Mr. Connelly."

Brooke just looked at me and said, "Calm down Joey."

I stared at the nurse and said, "I'll finish up here. You can leave." That's when I promised Brooke that I would be the only one to clean her.

"That's impossible. What about Sara... work. You can't be here all the time."

"Watch me," I said and she stood quietly. She knew I was upset, but I could also tell she was most comfortable with me cleaning and changing her.

"Do you mind emptying the basket with the gowns and towels? It's pretty full. Also, can I get some more gowns for the room?" I asked the two nurses currently manning the station. They nodded and went to the room. I walked over to the bathroom out in the hall and stood in front of the mirror. As I took off the bloody shirt, I stared at myself and didn't realize how thin I'd become. I used to fill in this flannel shirt; I couldn't even remember the last time I had eaten. Now the flannel shirt just hung off me. I ran hot water over the stain on the shirt and dabbed soap on it. I scrubbed and scrubbed so hard and so fast that I didn't realize I was putting a hole in the shirt. I stopped, out of breath, and looked in the mirror again, staring at what seemed like another person. *How am I going to get through this?* I slowly crumpled to the floor, leaned against the door, and wept like baby.

I sat in the chair watching her sleep, thinking of the times we laid in the same bed. I truly missed those days. As the blanket rose up and down with each breath she took, I watched and started to dose off, reminding myself that I needed to pick up Sara from Carroll's tomorrow. I woke up a bit startled hearing a commotion outside the room. It sounded like it was coming from next door, Jimmy's room. Jimmy was this sweet, twelve-year-old boy who had leukemia. He'd been Brooke's next door neighbor for the last three months, room number 408. I looked at my watch, it was 6:15 in the morning. *What the heck is going on?* All I could hear was the nurses scrambling and a bunch of beeps and sirens. Then I heard Joanne's voice screaming, "NO, NO, NOT MY BABY!" It echoed throughout the hospital. By then, I was wide awake and realized what was happening. I jumped up and looked over at Brooke. She had her eyes closed, but was awake; I could tell because she had one hand over her mouth and the other over her heart and tears were rolling down her cheeks. I just stood there; I didn't know what to do.

We had gotten to know the Andersons pretty well. They were a middle-aged couple in their fifties—both divorced and met, of all places, at a hockey game. Joanne was already divorced when they met, but Jim wasn't. They fell in love and decided it was never too late to take a second shot at true love. Well, that's what they said. They must have told us the hockey game story a hundred times. Jim was visiting his brother, Mark, and went to a hockey game where he met Joanne. As Jim tells us, after that he never looked back. They got married a few months later, once Jim's divorce was finalized, and bought a house here in Seattle. Within a year, she was pregnant at forty-one years old. She told Brooke and I that Jimmy was a miracle baby because she had been married for fifteen years before and never had children. She said they had tried, but it never happened. I walked over to Brooke, took her hand from her heart, and held it. She looked up at me and knew what I was thinking as I watched the lines bleep on her heart monitor. We knew Jimmy was on borrowed time, especially these last few weeks. He had gotten to the point where he could barely speak—and this kid was a chatter box when he first got here. We just looked at each other, an unspoken truth filled the room— like we both knew that she too was on borrowed time.

Jim had two daughters from his previous marriage—which Brooke and I had the pleasure of meeting, Mary and Rose. Mary was a twenty-year-old college student, who worked part time at Starbucks. She was a sweetheart, very bubbly and talkative and seemed fine with Joanne. Rose, on the other hand, was three years younger than Mary, and you could tell that she harbored feelings of resentment toward Joanne; but they both lit up with joy when they were around Jimmy.

The first time I met Jimmy, he was racing around the hall in a wheel-chair while the nurses were trying to catch him. Chasing him down the hall, they yelled, "Little Mr. Anderson, please stop horse-playing! You're in no shape to be horsing around!" As I walked down the hall from the elevator, amused by the spirit this kid had, I could hear him yelling back, "Catch me if you can!" Then, he was headed my way and would have run me over if I hadn't caught the wheel with my shoe.

"Whoa there cowboy," I said while the nurses caught up and grabbed the handles on the chair. He looked up at me with freckled cheeks and a huge grin on his face.

"What's up?" he giggled.

"What's up?" I asked back. "Well, let's start with your name cowboy."

"Jimmy," he replied, breathing heavily from all of the activity that just took place.

I extended my hand to him, "Joe. Nice to meet you Jimmy." He took my hand and shook it, then the nurses turned him around and rolled him back to his room. Later that evening, Brooke and I met the Anderson's as a whole, and boy were they a talkative bunch. That's when they told us that Jimmy was there for treatment of acute leukemia. It turns out that he had it when he was ten, and they were able to treat it with chemotherapy. He had been in remission until recently. They discovered that it came back in the lab results of his last check-up. They sounded so positive—the way they spoke— almost routine. Joanne waved her hand without a concern in the world when she said, "We will get through these treatments and have him home in two to three months, tops. Just in time for his birthday and summer camp."

Jimmy's eyes lit up when Joanne mentioned summer camp; he almost jumped out of his wheelchair. He shouted excitedly, "Yeah that's right! It's coming up in July, my birthday and summer camp. I can't wait to hang out with Ricky and Bobby. We're going to shoot bow and arrows and scare the girls at night in their dorm!" Joanne cut in imme- diately, "You will do no such thing young man." Jimmy just grinned at her. She couldn't help but smile lovingly at him as she patted his arm.

Joanne and Brooke started a conversation about church. I knew Brooke was going to bring it up sooner or later. She just loved helping out at the church and talking to people she felt needed God in their lives. I use to tell her, "You scared them off, you Jesus freak!" It was a nickname she did not care for. Joanne seemed to be open to the conversation; some people would just look at her funny or change the subject. Brooke wasn't pushy about it, she just had an unbreakable faith. This was when Jim started with the man talk. "So tell me Joe, what is it that you do for a living?"

I smiled and replied, "Well, it's a long story Jim." He smiled and raised his hand to gesture around us like, 'what else is there to do'. So, I told him that I had gone to college with the goal of becoming an architect. I was in my third year when I lost both my parents in a terrible car accident. His eyes saddened and he began to apologize. Joanne also overheard and did the same. I nodded my head and thanked them. It was always weird; it happened so long ago, and yet whenever it comes up in a conversation, people start apologizing like it just happened last week. Brooke smiled at me and blew me a kiss; she probably knew what I was thinking. I've said this once or twice to her over the years.

To break the short silence, I continued telling him about my job, "You see, my dad was a general contractor. He owned and ran a contracting business. When him and Mom died, I really didn't know what to do with the business. I also have a younger sister, Carroll. I actually wanted to sell the business, but Carroll refused and said that Dad loved to build things. She said, 'Joey don't you remember when Dad took us to that building on Kitsap Way that was mid-build?' Our father had gently unrolled the blueprints like they held some kind of secret, and we both looked at them confused by the complexity. She was nine and I was thirteen at the time. We just stared at the blueprints with all the lines and numbers and penciled-in notes in Dad's hand writing. He then looked at both of us and said, 'My children, there is nothing more gratifying in the world than taking an empty piece of land that someone has given up on, and giving it purpose—to build something that means something for someone else; a home for a family, a school where children can learn. There are so many possibilities, and it all starts with this'. He bent over and picked up a hammer and a nail. He said, 'God blessed these hands with a talent for building.' Then, gave us the biggest smile. With tears in her eyes, my sister insisted that we not sell."

I smiled at Jim, crossed my arms across my chest, and concluded, "So, here I am, a general contractor. I dropped out of college and took over my dad's business—well me and my sis, Carroll. Although, sometimes it seems like she runs it all." I broke out laughing and he joined in. From then on, we had get-togethers in either Jimmy's room or Brooke's. Sometimes, they would ask if we could keep an eye on Jimmy if they had to run out and take care of some stuff, or if Jim had to call his partners. Turns out that Jim was a successful guy; he was a part owner of five companies that made golf balls—they were spread out across the United States, including some sales in Europe. But, since Jimmy had gotten sick, he had 'semi-retired' and let his partners run the day-to-day business, with a few phone calls here and there.

Jimmy definitely was one-of-a-kind. When his parents weren't around, he would ask me all kinds of questions—like: when was the first time I kissed a girl, how did I think the Seahawks were going to do this year. He told me that his dad takes him to a game every year; he even talked about Brooke and I going with him and his dad one day. He always wanted me to go to his room to play doubles on his X-Box; his favorite game was Medal of Honor, and when he won, he would throw his hands up and shout, "What, What! That's right, this is Jimmy's house!" I would just laugh and agree that he was the man. He would break into this huge grin that made his freckles look bigger.

One day, he went crazy when he caught me parking my 1969, cherry red Chevy Cheval in the parking lot. Jimmy begged his mom to let him take a ride in my car. I said I didn't mind, but she would say, "No, you can't leave the hospital. You could get sick or catch something. We can't take that chance." Jimmy would just make a pouty face and look at his dad for help. Jim would put his hands up in surrender and say, "I love you son, but that's one fight I would lose."

It turns out that, this time, the acute leukemia had gotten further into Jimmy's body. They were considering removing his spleen. Jim and Joanne jumped at it, "If it saves Jimmy," they said bluntly, "do it." When the doctors came back and said that it was beyond that, it was devastating news.

"You're not the best! We need the best. Get a specialist in here now!" Jim screamed. Joanne didn't stop him either; she held her husband's arm and stared at the doctor with disdain. All the doctor said was, "I wish there was something I could do to change this sir, but there isn't. If you want, I can get you another doctor."

"Well what the hell are you waiting for?" Jim spat. The doctor sighed and walked away. The conversation took place right outside Jimmy's room, so Brooke and I overheard the whole thing. This came eight days after our own bad news about Brooke's chemo not working. After that, Jim and Joanne were less talkative and would wave and say a quick 'hello' solemnly as they passed Brooke's room. Jimmy would still pop over when his parents went to do something or grab a bite. Jimmy would ask Brooke about the book she was always reading. She told him that it was the Bible. He tilted his head and asked, "What's it about?" Brooke smiled and began to tell him about God—how he created the Earth, Noah's ark, Moses, and God's beloved son, Jesus, who came to save us. All of these stories peaked his interest to the point that he would pop up every chance he got to hear more about this incredible man, Jesus, and how he healed people; and how, if you believed and had faith in him, when you left this world you would go to Heaven and be with him for eternity with no more pain or tears. Jimmy smiled at this news; Jimmy knew what death was. He was twelve and knew that he was dying, but hearing of Heaven made Jimmy feel better.

This didn't fare well with the other Andersons, however. Jimmy told Jim and Joanne, when they were crying by his bedside, "Don't cry

Mom and Dad. When I die, Jesus will come take me to Heaven, and I won't be in pain anymore." They knew immediately where he had heard this. Jim walked in to Brooke's room upset. I stood up when I saw the expression on his face.

"Who the hell do you think you are filling my son's head with these ideas? He's our son; don't go selling him a dream that doesn't exist." I was about to tell Jim to get the hell out of Brooke's room when she grabbed my wrist. I turned to look at her and she just smiled at me before replying to Jim, "I'm sorry you feel that way Jim. I really don't want to upset you or Joanne, and I certainly mean no harm to Jimmy. I know your family has received horrible news; how do you think he feels, knowing he's going to die? Even if you don't believe... let's say you're right, it's just a dream that doesn't exist, but if it makes him feel better, if he's less afraid knowing that there is a place called Heaven and there is a man named Jesus who will be there to take care of him, then what's the harm. This comforts him; wouldn't you rather him have these thoughts than those of not knowing what's next?" Jim unclenched his fist, put his head down, and allowed the tears to roll down his cheeks. I walked over to him, put my hand on his shoulder, and gave a reassuring squeeze in a gesture of understanding his anger. He lifted his head suddenly and shrugged off my hand from his shoulder, "If there is a God, or this Jesus, then why are they letting this happen to my boy?" Before Brooke could reply, he stormed out of the room.

Brooke held her Bible close to her chest, looked up towards the ceiling, and said, "God I know you're there. Please help the Andersons through this. I don't understand why this is happening or why you choose to take lives that have not lived long enough. I... I..." She just closed her eyes, not knowing what to say. I sat next to her bed and held her hand.

"Brooke, don't worry about it. You were just trying to make Jimmy feel better," I offered. She slowly turned her head to meet my eyes. Then, she threw a curve ball at me.

"How's your faith these days Joey?" I didn't know what to say. I didn't want to upset her; she was already in a fragile state. How could I tell her that I didn't want to hear about God right now—that I was upset with him too. I was familiar with God and the Bible long before I met Brooke; we always said grace and thanked God at the dinner table while I was growing up. I wouldn't say my family were devout Christians or anything like that, but I got more involved because of Brooke. Even then, Brooke would have to egg me on here and there to get me more involved with the church.

But right now, how do I tell her that I don't feel God here, and I haven't for a long time? Maybe Jim was right. Maybe it was just a dream. Why else would He be doing this to little Jimmy or my beautiful wife—taking her away from Sara and I? When our little girl was born, Brooke said, "God had given her to us." So now, how does that translate to Him taking Brooke away? Why would God do that, why? I sat there pondering these things in my head; Brooke noticed how long it took me to answer.

"Joey," she said breaking into my thoughts and looking at me a little worried.

"Of course my faith is strong. I pray every day." She relaxed and smiled. I hated lying to her, but I didn't want to tell her how I really felt.

The last time I spoke to Jimmy, he was sitting next to me in my red 1969 Chevy. Jim and Joanne finally came to talk to Brooke and I after 'the incident'—not about what was said; it never came up, so we didn't bother to mention it either. Jimmy still wanted to ride in my car. So, they came next door to ask. I guess they just wanted to give Jimmy some excitement since he had seemed so drained lately. I agreed immediately. Joanne and Jim stood there watching closely as I strapped Jimmy into the passenger seat. I jumped in the driver's seat and Jimmy looked at me with that famous grin plastered to his face.

"You ready cowboy?" I asked.

"Fire it up Joe!"

When I turned the ignition, the Chevy's engine came to life. *VVRROOM, VVRROOM.* Jimmy's eyes lit up. As I put it into gear, Joanne yelled over the hum of the engine, "Not too fast Joe!" I smiled and nodded to her as she looked at Jimmy and I with an expression of worry on her face. I drove off the hospital's parking lot, made a right, and hit the highway. We were ten minutes on the road when I turned to see Jimmy's expression; he had his eyes closed and his right arm out the window with his fingers spread wide open. Holding his arm as steady as he could, the wind kept pushing his hand back. He looked free as a bird just sitting there with his eyes closed and a smile on his face. It was like all the months in the hospital, the chemo, the pain, had all just melted away. I smiled and stared down the road. It was just Jimmy and I; no words were spoken, just the wind in our hair and the hum of the engine. It was almost like we were flying—both of us away from the hospital, leaving all the tears and the pain back there. I drank in that moment with Jimmy.

I was headed back to the hospital when Jimmy decided to say something, "Joe, you mind stopping somewhere before we get back to the hospital?"

"Jimmy you know we've been gone now for forty minutes. Your parents probably already put out a missing persons' report on you, and I'll have the police on me at any moment."

He smiled, "Just for a sec…" So, I pulled over, turned off the car, and asked him what was up. He just stared out the window as the cars passed by. Then, he knocked the wind right out me, "Joe is everything Brooke told me true? Will I go to Heaven? I won't be afraid when I die if Jesus takes me to live with him in Heaven." Jimmy watched me closely; the kid trusted me, and I knew he looked up to me. How do I break his heart and tell him that I'm not speaking to God at the moment? That I'm upset with Him, if there is a Him. I looked at Jimmy's face as he started to look frightened by my slow response.

"Of course Jimmy. God is everywhere. Heaven is right here; it's so close you can almost touch it. My uncle Carl is there."

He looked at me inquisitively, and then asked another out-of-the-box question, "When your uncle Carl died, how exactly does it happen? How did he get to Heaven?" The kid really had me stumbling to choose the next words out of my mouth carefully. Suddenly, my memory hit me; when my dad's brother, Uncle Carl, died in the Marines in a training exercise, I was seven years old at the time. I stood next to my dad, holding his hand, and flinched every time they fired their weapons in the twenty-one-gun salute at the funeral. I asked my dad the same question. 'Where did Uncle Carl go?' My dad replied, "To Heaven son."

As I watched them lower his coffin into the ground, I looked at my dad and said, "Heaven is in the ground?" My dad looked at me and broke into a half-smile.

He kneeled down next to me, put his hands on my shoulders, and said, "No son, Heaven is all around us. It's in our hearts and our soul."

Then, I threw a curve ball at my dad, "What's a soul?"

He gave me a huge smile and told me, "A soul is who we are. It's what makes us... well... us." My dad looked around and saw some bushes nearby. He stood up, held my hand, and walked me over to the bushes and plants. He looked intently and pointed at a caterpillar and some cocoons hanging off a few of the small branches. "Joey, you see that caterpillar? It's living its life, and it's a brief one. It eats, sleeps, and lives; then, it's time for a change. So, it wraps itself up in a cocoon, and when the time comes, it emerges as a butterfly—to live a new life where it soars above everything, looking beautiful and flying gracefully through the sky. This is the same thing that happened to your Uncle Carl. His life has ended here on Earth, in the body that's being lowered into the ground. But, just like the caterpillar, that body was Uncle Carl's cocoon. His soul is the same as the butterfly—when it leaves the cocoon, only the soul is left to fly to Heaven to live there with God and the angels."

I told Jimmy the same thing. He seemed satisfied with that answer, so I fired up the engine. I was surprised I even remembered that story. My dad always had a way of explaining things; it had me thinking about all my issues with faith and what was happening to Brooke. When I pulled up to the hospital, I told Jimmy, "Don't tell your parents about our conversation."

He smiled, "I know. It'll be our secret." Before he stepped out of the car, he looked back at me and said, "See you later caterpillar; this butterfly is out." Seeing the huge grin on his freckled face, Joanne asked, "What are you talking about? Did you see a butterfly?" She looked around as she was helping him out of the car. Jimmy and I laughed out loud. Jim came around and shook my hand, "Thanks Joe." Before he turned to walk away, he looked at me and added, "I'm sorry about what I said to you and Brooke. If there is a God, I hope he takes care of my boy." I shook his hand and nodded.

That was the last time I spoke to Jimmy. He slipped into a coma two days ago, and now he's gone. It breaks my heart standing here hearing them next door. I can literally hear their hearts breaking with each sob. I wiped Brooke's tears away from her cheek. She pointed at my eyes, and I realized a few tear drops had made their escape down my cheek as well. I wiped them furiously with the back of my hand. We didn't say anything—just stood there in silence, holding hands and listening to Jim and Joanne beg for Jimmy to come back.

CHAPTER 2

The Space Needle

WHEN I LEFT THE HOSPITAL to pick up Sara, Jimmy's room was empty. Jim and Joanne had followed Jimmy's body down to where they kept the people who've passed on. We overheard them arguing with the hospital staff after they were told that they couldn't follow Jimmy. In the end, the hospital gave in. We said no good-byes; they were in so much pain, we just stood right next door in silence. They left sobbing and holding onto Jimmy's hospital bed as the nurse rolled him down the hall to a service elevator.

On my way out that morning, I stopped in front of Jimmy's room and looked in. My heart was in my throat as I whispered into the room, "You the man Jimmy." I tapped the wall twice and left.

As I drove to the ferry station to take the forty-five-minute ride to Downtown Bremerton, I wondered how Brooke felt. She was getting weaker and weaker by the day. Was she frightened? Sometimes, she didn't look scared at all—as if she had come to accept what was coming. I was scared to death. There were times when I couldn't accept what's happening. It all seemed like some bad dream that I couldn't wake from. Then, my mind went to Sara, *what about her?* I closed my eyes at the thought of her growing up without Brooke in her life. It had been a week since I'd seen, or even held, my daughter. The hospital doesn't allow children, let alone toddlers, in the cancer care unit. We've had many heavy discussions, sometimes arguments—more on my side, if anything—with the hospital when it came to this rule. I would tell them, "That's her mother! You can't keep a child from her mother, it's not right!" They always replied, "Mr. Connelly, it's for the safety of your daughter This floor has a lot of ill people and the chemotherapy room is also on this floor. You wouldn't want her around these types of medications. Not only that Mr. Connelly, the hospital is liable if your daughter were to get sick from anything related to the treatments for our cancer patients. We do apologize sir." Brooke looked at me and said, "Joey its fine. Even though it breaks my heart that I can't see her, I wouldn't want her in danger." I sighed, I guess she was right. Neither one of us was willing to put our daughter at risk.

I drove up to the teller, paid for the ferry ride, got my ticket, and followed the line of cars onto the ferry. I sat in the car watching all of the other people get out of their cars—some on their way to work in Bremerton, or back home from a night shift in downtown Seattle, all rushing for a seat inside the heated ferry and a cup of coffee. I looked at my watch, *Damn, it's 7:30. I'm running an hour late.* Then I remembered, I never did call Carroll to tell her that I was coming for Sara. *I'll call her when I'm on the ferry and have her get Sara ready, but I gotta make it quick.* The hospital was allowing us to bring Sara today for two hours, starting at 10:00 am. Once I reached Bremerton, I'd have a twenty-minute drive to Belfair, where we live—*which should put me at Carroll's house by 8:40,* I concluded. I looked around. Everyone was out of their cars already. I suddenly felt like I could go for a cup of coffee myself. I jumped out of the car to head in when a cold breeze hit me. Man it was cold! I turned around and grabbed my jacket before closing the door and locking it. It was mid-March and getting on the waters of Puget Sound made the temperatures drop even lower. I threw on my jacket, lifted the collar, and jogged up the stairs that led inside the ferry.

I walked in and glanced around. Everyone was in their own world. A lady looked out the window drinking her coffee while a couple in their early twenties snuggled up to each other looking at a cell phone. Others read books or were on a laptop punching away at the keys, all of course with a cup of coffee. I looked at the coffee machine and saw two people in front of it. I thought, *Good, no line.* As I headed over, one of the two had already gotten their coffee and walked away. I stood behind an elderly man who seemed like he was having difficulty making up his mind on what type of coffee he wanted. The coffee machine had different buttons with multiple choices. I looked over his shoulder wondering what the holdup was. The man noticed me and began to turn with a somewhat quirky side-step shuffle, almost like he couldn't really lift up his feet.

I turned, looking out the window nonchalantly, when he said, "Young man..." I looked left and right, then pointed at myself. "Yes you," he answered. He was shaking a dollar in his left hand and pointing at it with his right hand. He had to be in his late seventies, maybe eighty. He had on what seemed like an old fisherman's hat, but it still had the price tag on it. He wore a sports coat with patches on the elbows, pants that were almost chest height, and a shirt that read 'I love Seattle'. He stared at me through probably the thickest eye glasses I've ever seen, which made his eyes seem bigger than they actually were. He said, "Young man, I can't for the life of me figure out where to put this dollar to get a cup of joe. Can you help me out? He had a weird accent, and I knew right away that he was from out of town. I took the dollar from his hand, "Sure, not a problem." I slid the dollar in the slot and asked him what he wanted. He looked at me and asked what his choices were. *Are you kidding me?* I thought silently. He stood there staring at me, waiting for me to tell him the choices.

I kind of stammered, "Umm...w...well there's regular, caramel, mocha, and French vanilla." All the while, I was looking around thinking, *is this really happening?* He had his hands interlocked over his stomach while I was reading him his options.

He finally said, "That one." I stopped, "The French vanilla?"

"Yup," He confirmed.

I looked at him. "You're sure?" I asked, being a little sarcastic. He looked at me, suddenly a little worried about his decision.

"Hold on," he said and began to walk away with that quirky shuffle of his. His walk kind of resembled a penguin's. My mouth dropped open; my sarcasm had backfired. *Is this guy serious?* I leaned against the machine thinking, *all I wanted was a cup of coffee. I didn't want to talk to or deal with anyone, how did I get stuck with this old man.* He showed up with an elderly woman, about the same age, as they both shuffled towards me. His elbow was high and her hand was resting through his arm. She wore a long dress with a blue rain jacket that had a photo of the Space Needle. Her hat said 'Seattle', also with the price tag hanging from it. They stood in front of me—the old woman with a smile on her face; the old man with his chin held high and a proud look on his face.

He said, "Young man, this is my beautiful wife, who the cup of joe is for."

I leaned forward to shake her hand, "Nice to meet you."

She looked at me with a big smile and kind eyes, then nudged him in the ribs, "Where's your manners Harry?"

"Oh, oh... what's your name young man?"

"Joe," I smiled.

"Joe this is my wife, Rose," He once again referred to the elderly woman with a slight bow.

She nodded her head, "It is a pleasure to meet you Joe."

"What da ya know, a fella named Joe helping me get a cup of joe," the old man said with a chuckle as he snapped his fingers.

Rose smiled at him, "Oh Harry, you still make me laugh after all these years." He looked at her through those thick eyeglasses with loving eyes.

"My love, I do it all for you."

She patted him on his arm and looked back at me. "So what seems to be causing all the fuss over here?"

"Well, Ma'am, your husband wasn't sure what coffee you wanted," I replied. She looked at the machine, assessed that the money was in because there was a flashing 'select' signal on the machine, and let go of her husband's arm so that she could walk over and push the button that said 'regular'.

Rose looked at me, smiling with those kind eyes and said, "Thanks for all your help Joe." She turned to Harry, gave him a kiss on the cheek, and said, "I'll wait back at our seats with the table." As she shuffled away, he stared at her with pride and a smile.

He then turned to me, "Ain't she somethin?"

I smiled at the old man, "She sure is Harry." He grabbed the coffee when it was done and started to walk off. "Hold on Harry, you need a coffee lid," I said, handing him the lid.

He gave me an earnest look, "You're a good man Joe. You know, in New York, I probably could have stood there for an hour and no one would have helped me."

"So you're from New York? Ha, I thought you had a strange accent."

"Strange? Sonny I'm as smooth talkin as old blue eyes himself." He threw me for a second. Then, I realized he meant Frank Sinatra. I only knew that because my father was a Frank Sinatra fan and referred to himself as the Chairman of the Board for old blue eyes.

"So Harry, how long you two been in Seattle?" I inquired.

"Got here two days ago. We are visiting our grandson and his family." Then Harry looked up like he had a thought but couldn't quite put his finger on it. After a brief pause, he continued, "Well, maybe more than just visiting. You see Joe, some big shot corporation came in and started making offers for the homes in our neighborhood. They said they're putting up one of those dang super malls. I didn't want to sell. That was the home where we raised our children; we've lived there for fifty years. They said we had no choice, that the county agreed, and they gave us a settlement. It broke my beautiful Rose's heart to let go of our home. I damn near took a swing at the man when he came with the settlement papers, but Rose said it wasn't worth it. She knew I would've hurt the fella; I used to be a boxer in the Navy, ya know..." I smiled as he held the coffee in one hand and slowly threw a jab with the other. "They took our house, but you know what Joe, Rose and I together is home."

"How long have you and Rose been married?"

He turned to me with that proud look again and answered, "Fifty-three years Joe, and I thank God for every day with her. Every morning that I wake up with her next to me, I look up and say, 'Thanks Big

Guy'." He winked at me and shuffled off. I got my coffee and looked at Harry and Rose sitting in one of the booths—his arm around her, smiling while she drank her coffee. My heart crumbled as I thought, *I'll never have that with Brooke… the chance to grow old together.* A stabbing pain hit my stomach; my eyes began to water, and I looked around wondering if anyone had noticed. I headed outside to the deck. As I stepped out, I was hit with a freezing cold wind. I didn't care, though. I walked to the edge of the railing, letting the freezing wind hit my face. It actually felt good; it numbed me. I watched as the seagulls flew side-by-side with the ferry, whining and squawking, as mists of water seemed to be all around me. I couldn't help but smile as I thought about Harry; he was a character. He seemed so happy. He thanked God every day. *I can't seem to get away from God,* I thought to myself almost bitterly. *He seems to be in almost every conversation I have, even outside the hospital.* In the hospital, you get used to hearing about God and prayers because people fear being sick or dying.

I watched downtown Seattle get smaller and smaller the further we got from it. The one structure that stood out from all the buildings was the Space Needle. I remember meeting Brooke across the street. I was doing a remodel on a restaurant right across from the Space Needle. The new owners of the restaurant had us put in large windows that curved into the roof; so, when dining there, you had a full view of the Space Needle. I was twenty-three years old and running my dad's company. My mom and dad had already been gone a few months. So here I was, this twenty-three-year-old college dropout, running a construction company without out a clue as to what I was doing. Thank God for Phil, my dad's general foreman. I've known Phil for most of my life. As a kid, I called him Uncle Phil; as I got older, I dropped the 'uncle' part.

I was stumbling off the truck carrying a five-gallon bucket of drywall mix when she caught my eye—this girl walking down the sidewalk, headed my way. She was wearing a yellow sun dress with a soft blue sweater. Her hair was in a ponytail that bounced with every step she took. As she got closer, I saw those big, beautiful green eyes; I swear my heart literally skipped a beat. She caught me staring at her and put her head down with a shy smile. She was within five steps of me; I continued to stare, almost hypnotized by her. Not paying attention to where I was walking, I tripped over a bag of cement. I tried to steady my feet, but I was going down fast and hard, so I used the bucket of drywall mix to break my fall. When it hit the floor, it busted open as my body weight fell into it. *'Poof'* a cloud of white powder filled the air. I just laid there, left blinded and coughing by the white cloud of dry wall mix. Suddenly, I heard a voice ask, "Are you okay?" I could make out the silhouette of the girl and knew that it was her voice asking me through the white cloud. I coughed two more times as the powder began to settle. Looking at her, I was completely embarrassed as I laid there covered in dry wall. She stood there looking at me worriedly. I was speechless when she reached out her hand to help me up.

I was finally able to untie my tongue, "Yeah I'm good." I grabbed her hand and at the same time pushed myself up. I stood up rubbing the back of my neck, still embarrassed by what just happened. I looked around and said somewhat loudly to the crew working inside the restaurant, "Which one of you guys left a bag of cement out here?"

Then, Phil's voice cut in, "You did dummy." The green-eyed girl let out a laugh.

"Oh yeah…" was all I could say. I gave her a sheepish smile, feeling even more embarrassed.

"Joe we gotta lot to get done in here. Either you get in here to learn, or go to the shop and see if our order of steel beams came in." Phil added.

"I'll go check on the beams Phil." I said, never taking my eyes off her. He looked out the door at the green-eyed girl and I just staring at each other—her with a smile on her face and me red-faced and embarrassed.

"Yeah, you do that kid. We will take care of what we got going on in here." Phil said smiling.

She spoke first, "Well I guess you're good so I'll let you get going to see about those beams." She turned and started to walk away. I just stood there watching her go. My heart was pounding in my chest; I just couldn't let her leave like that. *What if I never see her again?* My mind raced for reasons to go after her with something to say. When I saw her stop at the street light waiting for it to turn green, I knew that this was my chance. I jogged over to the corner where she was waiting. I knew she saw me coming, but she never turned her head. She just stood there with this smile on her face. *That's a good sign,* I thought. When I came along the side of her, she still didn't look at me—just kept her head looking straight on with a smile on her face. I was going to say something, but I didn't. I turned and looked straight across the street with a smile on my face too. The light turned green, she began to cross, and I did the same. Both of us were smiling, yet still didn't acknowledge each other. The whole time I was thinking of what to say.

Here I was, walking side-by-side with this girl; I have no idea where she's going, but I can't bring myself to leave her side. I realized that she was headed right into the Space Needle building. She paid the thirteen dollars, got her ticket, and continued on. She had the exact amount. I didn't want to lose her. I asked for the ticket and gave the girl at the register twenty dollars.

The cashier asked me, "Is everything alright sir?" The entire time my gaze was transfixed on the green-eyed girl. She repeated her question again, "Is everything alright sir?"

I finally broke my trance and looked at the girl, "Yeah, why do you ask?"

"Sir, you're covered in white powder. All I can see are your eyes and your lips move when you speak." I forgot that I looked like Casper the friendly ghost.

"Uh yeah, I'm working across the street… spilled a little drywall mix on myself, but I'm fine." She was holding my ticket and staring at me.

"I'm not sure I can let you in like that sir." I looked at this eighteen, maybe nineteen, year-old girl who took her job a little too seriously.

"You see that girl who is about to get onto the elevator?"

"Yeah," she said, looking over to where I was pointing.

"That's my girlfriend. I'm about to propose to her when we get to the top."

"Awww, in that case let me get your change."

The green-eyed girl was almost at the elevator. "Screw it, keep the change!" I said and grabbed my ticket. Speed walking to the elevator, I was right behind her when she stepped in. I slid right in and stood in the far corner looking out the glass window of the elevator. We were the only two in the elevator. I could see her in the reflection staring at me with a puzzled look on her face.

Once again, she spoke first, "So should I be worried that I have a giant powdered donut stalking me?"

"Beautiful and funny," I said with a laugh. I turned around to look at her, put out my arm, and said, "You're safe pretty lady, but if you're craving a powdered donut, go ahead… help yourself." She looked at me with widened eyes and we both broke out laughing. We got to the top and stepped out together. She looked at me and smiled. I smiled back.

We still didn't say much, but our eyes kept making contact. We headed

outside and I walked over to the edge, looking through the bars—which

I suspected were there to prevent anyone from taking a nose dive off the

edge. I turned to the green-eyed girl, "You wanna know something? I've

lived in Washington my whole life and have never been up here before."

"Really?"

"Yeah really," I said, trying to give her my winning smile. I was still

fairly oblivious to how I looked until I saw my reflection in the large

windows of the inside concession area. *Whoa damn, I do look like a giant*

powdered donut. "I'm surprised you're even giving me the time of day."

"Well, I saw you before the powder incident. You were carrying the

bucket on your shoulder with your cut off shirt and your blue jeans."

"Ahhh you were checking me out."

She blushed, "No I wasn't."

"You totally were."

She smiled, "Let's get rid of the powder."

"How do you suggest we do that?"

"Just follow me." We began to walk around to the other side of the

top of the Space Needle, and as soon as we came around the other side,

the wind was so strong that you almost had to lean into it. She looked at

me smiling and said, "Hold your hands straight out and take a few more steps." We moved closer to the edge; all the powder started blowing off of me into the air. I could see the wind carrying it up until it dissipated. I ran my fingers through my hair, shaking my head almost like I do when I'm taking a shower. As I finished patting the rest of the powder off me, I turned to look at her. She had undone her ponytail and stood with her arms out and her eyes closed. I stood there watching her. Her hair flowed in the wind and her blue sweater now took on the appearance of a cape flowing behind her. The sun dress clung tightly to her body, showing off her womanly curves. I was mesmerized by her, and I didn't even know her name. I leaned against the railing watching her. "What are you looking at?" she asked. I thought, *how does she know I was looking at her? Her eyes are closed.*

I said, "You."

"Why?"

"You seem so at peace."

She smiled, "I love it up here." She still hadn't opened her eyes. She finally turned to look at me, "I come up here at least three times a month to clear my head of all the realities of life. I talk to God, my mom, and enjoy the view." I thought to myself, *whoa maybe she's a little off.*

"So, um… you talk to God? Does he ever talk back?" I looked at her quizzically. Her smile quickly disappeared; her green eyes looked like emeralds with tints of red as if lit by fire. I stood up straight, feeling her anger. She relaxed her look, bent over, picked up her purse, and began walking away. I took four giant steps and grabbed her arm, "Whoa, whoa... what happened?"

"I'm sorry I brought you up here," she said yanking her arm away.

"Why? What did I say?"

"You mocked me. I saw the look on your face; you were thinking that I'm a quack of some sort."

"No, not at all! It just threw me when you said you talk to God."

"You don't pray?" She asked. I paused and thought about the question. I remembered going to church on Sundays with my parents; it was a Catholic church and after the sermon the priest would say, 'let us pray'. Everyone would bow their heads, so I did the same, but the whole time I was thinking about how I couldn't wait until church was over so that I could go play with my friends.

"Well," I said, "when I was a kid, I went to church and prayed a few times." She burst out laughing. "Hey who's mocking who now?" She wiped her eyes; they had watered because she was laughing so hard. She got quiet and looked deeply into my eyes; I was speechless again.

"No, God does not speak back to me—not literally anyway. But I feel his presence when I'm up here in the air; the wind, the beauty of his creation." She walked back over to the railing, "Look... you see how everything is perfectly set? The mountains... the water... the trees." At first I was looking at the structures, the buildings, and thought, *men built this*, but after she pointed out everything else, I started to see what she was saying.

"Yes, you're right. It is beautiful." She smiled at me. I wanted to ask another question, but this time, I knew to tread softly. "May I ask you a question?"

Without looking at me, she just gazed out towards the water and said, "Yes."

"You mentioned your mom. I take it she's..." I paused.

"Passed on," she finished for me.

"Yes," I almost whispered.

She looked, "Yes, my beautiful mom has been gone from this world for ten years now."

"I'm so sorry to hear that." I didn't ask how. I know what it's like to relive that question. We both stood there looking out in silence. I thought about how peaceful it was up here. I turned my eyes back to her, wanting to know more about her. I yearned for it, but I didn't want to scare her off. I didn't like bringing it up because the pain of losing my mom and dad was still fresh. I looked out at the view as gusts of wind blew at us; something told me to tell her. "I recently lost both my parents... four months ago."

It was her turn to cast her eyes in my direction, "I'm sorry." She touched my hand while I was holding onto the railing; it sent a warm sensation throughout my body. Our eyes met, and I smiled and nodded. We stood there for another ten minutes, not saying anything, just looking out at the view. It was relaxing and peaceful. I understood why she came up here to get away from the fast pace of life. As I looked down, I saw the ant-sized people walking quickly from point A to B and cars zooming through the streets, all in a hurry. "I gotta get going," she said finally. I felt a slight ache in my stomach; I didn't want this moment to end, and I didn't know why. There was just something about her—just being around her made me feel better about life; it eased the pain of losing my parents. I just wanted to be near her.

"Uh, um... wait... I don't even know your name. How will I see you again?" I said, stumbling over my words.

She smiled, "Are you sure you want to? I talk to God, remember? Didn't that freak you out?"

I returned her smile and pointed two fingers at her, "Not literally though." She laughed. Oh how I loved the sound of her laugh. She began putting her hair up in a ponytail again. I stood there watching her in awe as she had the band in her mouth—tugging on her hair, pulling it back, holding it with one hand, and grabbing the band with her other hand, magically slipping it through her hair. She quickly wrapped it twice, patted the sides of her hair and said, "There, I'm good to go."

"So where is it you gotta go?"

"Back to school." I froze for a second, thoughts racing.

"Not high school I hope…" I replied. She broke out laughing again.

"No silly, I go to college here."

"Where?"

"Pacific University," she answered. I told her that I drive by there all the time.

"Third avenue right?"

"Yeah, that's the one." She slowly started to head inside toward the elevator. I still wasn't any nearer to getting any actual personal information from her; heck, I hadn't even gotten her name yet.

As I walked by her side, I asked, "Well, in case you've been dying to know, my name is Joe."

"It's nice to meet you Joe," she smiled as she said it and kept walking. I'm walking next to this girl, still debating on how crazy she actually is, but I can't bring myself to leave her side.

"Doesn't that info make you want to tell me something?"

"Tell you what?" she asked innocently. This girl was driving me nuts.

"Your name," I said a little exasperated.

"I don't really know you," she answered as we stepped into the elevator that took us back down to the realities of life.

"Really? I followed you up here, shared a special moment with you; I… I need to see you again." She smiled at my confession, seeing my desperation.

She paused in thought. "Most guys get your name, your number, you go out with them and then all they want to do is get in your pants, and if they don't they magically forget your number. Joe you are so cute, and believe me, as hard as it is for me to say it, I just don't have the time to play those games. I'm really busy with school and I have a year and a half until I graduate. I'm midway through this semester, and I really need to stay focused. I'm sorry you wasted your time with me today. Hopefully that man doesn't fire you for not checking on those beams." There was sadness in her eyes as she looked at me. The elevator came to a stop. My mind raced, *it can't end like this. I gotta see her again.* She walked out, smiled at me, and said, "Thanks for an interesting afternoon Joe, I won't forget it." Then, she turned and walked away. I stood there dumfounded, in shock. *Did that just happen?* I've dated a lot of girls in my time, especially in college, and when I approached them, they were eager to go out with me. I've never really had a problem meeting girls. I stood there baffled. When I looked up, she was already across the street, walking passed the restaurant where I worked. I ran to the stop light; it was red. *Damn she's getting away!* I looked right and left, then bolted across the street, almost getting run over by a red Jetta. The guy in the car honked angrily at me as I jumped out of the way. I ran passed the restaurant.

Phil stepped out and yelled at me as I ran passed, "What the hell are you doing Joe?"

"Can't talk now Phil." I yelled back. I caught up to her and slowed down as I walked by her side. I tried to calm my breathing so as not to let her know that I was chasing her down the street, but of course, she already knew.

"You really want to see me that bad that you almost got yourself killed?" she said hitting me on the arm.

"Oh that that guy? He was speeding; I think he ran a red light."

She smiled, "More like *you* ran the red light." I smiled back.

"So what does a guy gotta do to get your name or see you again?" She stopped walking and stared at me. "I can dodge cars all day if you want." I took a step in the street as a car zoomed by. She grabbed my arm.

"Are you crazy?" she said, as she pulled me back on the side walk. She stood there, her eyes on fire again.

"So what will it be?" I asked, folding my arms across my chest.

She smiled a little devilishly, "Alright Joe, I'll play your game. If you're serious about seeing me again, you know where my college is. We have a beautiful church on campus; service starts at 9:00 am on Sunday. I'll be waiting by the large white pillars on the left at 8:45, and if you're not there by 8:50, then I guess it wasn't meant to be." She turned and started walking away.

"Church? Why not breakfast, lunch, or dinner?"

"Church Joe," she said without turning around.

"It's Thursday! I hate having to wait till Sunday to see you," I yelled after her. "Wait!" She stopped and turned around.

"Joe I gotta go."

"I know, I know, but you still haven't told me your name?" She gave me a big beautiful smile.

"When I see you Sunday, you can have my name." She blew me a kiss and walked away. I just watched her leave until she disappeared into the crowd of people, thinking, *I can't wait to see her on Sunday.*

Sunday Morning, I got up at 6:00 am. I was excited. I woke up smiling and humming Benny and the Jets by Sir Elton John. It was stuck in my head. Phil and I had gone to a local pub the night before for a drink after leaving one of the work sites.

He walked over to the jute box and looked at me smiling, "Do you remember this song kid?" He put the money in the box and a familiar song came blasting out the speakers. I smiled as I heard the pounding of the piano, *Dun Dun Dun, Dun ta ta da, Dun Dun*; then the lyrics, *'hey kids shaking loose together the spot light hitting something that's been known to change the weather, so stick around'*. By this point, everyone in the pub had joined in mumbling the rest of the lyrics because we really didn't know what he was saying. But, we all waited for, *'Benny, Benny, Benny, and the Jets, Dun Dun ta ta da'*. There were about fifteen people in the pub, but it sounded like a hundred as everyone sang along. It was a good time. This was one of my parents' favorite songs. When I was a kid, they always talked about the Elton John concert. Phil had gone with them on a double date. They would always play this song at family get-togethers, and we would all sing along. It made me miss my mom and dad, a lot. Those were great memories.

As I hummed the tune, I put on an old pair of sweats and one of my old college sweatshirts. I tied my shoe strings and stepped out onto the porch. *Wow*, it was a beautiful morning. The sun was just peeking over the mountains, the air was crisp, and it wasn't raining today, which is weird because the day I met the green-eyed girl it was nice and sunny too. But, the entire rest of the week was pouring rain; now, the day I get to see her again, it's gorgeous. As I stretched, getting ready for my run, I smiled and thought, *this is fate.*

I finished up my run, and looked at my watch—6:40. I knew that I needed to hurry. I ran upstairs, jumped in the shower, jumped out, and started rummaging through my closet. *What do I where to church?* I hadn't been to church since I was a kid. I remembered my dad would wear a suit when we did go, so I thought that should impress her. I found an old jacket and tie, threw on some slacks and looked in the mirror. *Not bad if I do say so myself*, I thought, winking at the mirror. I didn't drive the truck. I pulled out of the garage in my dad's 1969 cherry red Cheval. As I turned the key, the roar of the engine came to life. I smiled, remembering how my dad spent many days under the hood of this car. I drove off thinking of the girl that had haunted my dreams since Thursday.

I drove up to the college campus, parked, and started wandering inside the school looking for any building that resembled a church with large white pillars. I asked a couple of guys I ran into on my way in where the church was. They looked at me a little funny and pointed me in the right direction. As I walked away, I looked at my jacket—did it have a stain I didn't see? I checked my tie; everything seemed to be in the right place. I thought, *whatever*. It was a large campus. Then, I came to the side of a large building, and the large white pillars she described caught my eye. She had told me to meet her on the left; I happened to be on the left side of the building. When I came around the building, there she was standing in front of the white pillar on the left. I looked at my watch; it was 8:39. I smiled, *she's waiting a little bit earlier than she said she would.* I straightened out my suit jacket, cleared my throat, and walked up behind her.

"Waiting for someone?" I whispered in her ear. She jumped.

"Hey, I wasn't expecting you to come in from behind the church."

"I'm full of surprises once you get to know me."

"I bet," she said with a smile. We stood there smiling at each other for a minute.

"So have I earned the right to know your name or shall I make one up for you?" I asked.

"That's not necessary. I'm Brooke," she extended her hand and I shook it.

"Joe," I told her again. We stood there shaking hands longer than a normal hand shake would last staring into each other's eyes, both of us with ridiculous smiles on our faces. We finally stopped and I noticed her looking me up and down; a huge smile came over her face. "What's so funny?"

"You," she giggled. I looked at myself thinking, *did I miss something on my suit? Maybe a tear?* I started inspecting my clothes again for anything I might have not seen. She began laughing out loud.

"Seriously, what?" I demanded. She stopped laughing and just smiled at me.

"You are so cute. There is nothing wrong with your suit; it's perfectly fine. It's just that, this is a relaxed environment, so no one dresses like that here for church." That's when I noticed what she was wearing: blue jeans, a yellow T-shirt, and sandals. Then, she grabbed my hand and said, "Let's go grab a seat." As we walked in, there were guys in T shirts, sweatshirts with their college logo on it, and even a few people in shorts and sweats. I felt like an idiot as I walked in; people looked at us smiling. *Damn, I tried to impress her and here I am the joke of her school church.* She saw the look on my face as I looked around feeling embarrassed. She stopped me, pulled my face to look at her, and said smiling, "You're fine. You actually look really handsome, don't worry." We found our seats and church began.

I watched her throughout the sermon; she was so engrossed in what was being said, and she prayed so intently. As I watched her praying, I thought, *God, she is beautiful. Thanks God for letting me meet her.* I wasn't a religious guy by any means, but no matter what brought us together I was happy for it.

Church was over. As we were walking out, we were so close that our hands kept touching. I saw this as my opportunity to slowly intertwine our fingers and hold her hand. She was looking around smiling, acting like she didn't notice as her fingers clenched mine. I smiled and thought, *I haven't been at peace with the world since my parents died.* And yet, walking here with her, holding hands, gave me some sort of calming comfort. We went to lunch and I told her how much I miss my parents and about dropping out of college to run my dad's company with my sister Carroll. She told me about how her mom passed away ten years ago; she was twelve years old.

"My mom died of cancer of the lymph nodes. It was tough on me; it still is."

"What about your dad?" I asked. She made a face.

"He left when I was three years old. I haven't seen him since."

"Oh, I'm sorry."

"Don't be. Mom was enough. She had enough love in her for the entire world. She was the greatest." I smiled. "On her death bed," she continued, "she was so positive, telling me how much she loved me and that she would always watch over me from Heaven." I thought to myself, *that explains the church thing.* "My mom believed in God so much that she told me to always be thankful, and not to just pray, but talk to God—tell him when your sad, frightened, or angry. I remember telling her at her bedside, 'I'm angry at God for trying to take you, Mom.

I need you. Why does he have to take you?' My mom wiped my tears, smiled, and said, 'It's alright to be angry; I sometimes ain't too happy with him for what's happening—not because of me, but because of you. But, it's not up to us to understand His plan; it's just about having faith. You know the picture on the wall at home, with the two sets of footprints in the sand, then there's only one set of footprints?' I nodded crying and she said, 'That means, when things get so bad that its almost humanly impossible to handle, that one set of footprints is when Jesus carries you. You might not know it, but he's carrying us both right now.' I just broke down as she hugged me, telling me how much she loved me." Brooke's eyes watered as she smiled at me, fighting back tears. I touched her hand.

"So who raised you?" I asked.

"My Nana and Pop... my grandparents," she said. "I'm from Montana. They were very supportive and loving, even when I chose to come out here to Pacific University; it's a Christian college.

"So you take this stuff seriously..."

She looked at me intently and replied, "Maybe my purpose for coming out here was to meet you and make you a believer."

I smiled, "Maybe."

From that day on we were inseparable. We always hung out and she would force me to go to church every Sunday. She met Carroll, and they hit it off right away. Brooke picked up calling me Joey from Carroll.

She said, "Joey, hmmm… I think I prefer that to Joe." She smiled and called me Joey from that point on. I would force her to go jogging with me; two or three times a month we would go to her favorite place at the top of the Space Needle—when it wasn't raining, of course. After seeing each other for four months, I asked her to move in with me. She had told me 'no' that entire month, but on the fifth month, she finally said 'yes'.

I lived in my parents' house by myself since they passed. My sister, Carroll, was living with her boyfriend, Richard. It was fun having Brooke around and having her in my bed. The first time we slept together, I remember how frightened she was. When I caught on that it was her first time, we had a few glasses of wine and listened to Sade's 'the Sweetest Taboo'; then, one thing led to another. She would always touch my chin with two fingers whenever she wanted to say that she loved me. I would do the same. It wasn't said, yet we both knew that we had fallen in love.

After our first night together, I asked her, "Are you alright with what happened last night? Isn't this like... against the rules?" I said, half smiling as I caressed her cheek. She looked at me smiling, all tangled up in the sheets with her hair disheveled. The way she looked in the mornings was so sexy.

"I know in my heart and soul that there was nothing wrong with last night," she answered as she touched my chin with two fingers. I was deeply in love with this girl, and I knew I couldn't live without her.

I took her to dinner at her favorite place, the Space Needle; it had a rotating restaurant at the top. I had to book the reservations a month in advance—turned out they were always booked. We had a great dinner; she smiled the whole time while we laughed and talked about life and friends. I repeatedly checked my pocket for the ring. Man I was nervous! Not nervous about asking her—if I was sure about anything in my life it was her. I just wasn't sure what her reaction would be. Dinner was done, I paid the check, and we went up to the next level that led outside. It was a beautiful evening; there were no clouds, and the stars were out, lighting up the sky. I glanced around; there were a few other couples up here. I was so nervous. We walked over to the edge, looking out at the city—at all the buildings lit up. It was quite a sight.

"So, I have a question for you," I said finally.

She looked at me, "Okayyy, what is it?" I had my hand in my pocket, holding onto the ring like my life depended on it. I turned so that I was facing her.

"Since the day I laid eyes on you, I knew I couldn't live without you." I kneeled down on one knee holding the ring as I locked eyes on her. "You mean more to me than the air I breathe. Would you be my wife?" Tears began coming down her cheeks. I heard some of the 'awww's in the background from the other couples.

"Yes, yes," she whispered. I took her left hand and slipped the ring on her finger. I stood up, touched her chin with two fingers; she touched mine with hers, and we both smiled and kissed with more passion than I had ever felt with anyone else.

CHAPTER 3

She's Gone

It's hard to believe that was eight years ago. It seemed almost like yesterday... *'HOOOONK'* The horn blew, bringing me back to reality—on the outside deck of the ferry, half frozen. The Captain started giving directions over the loud speaker, letting us know that we were nearing Bremerton. We were to get to our vehicles if we came on board with one and prepare for exiting the ferry. As I headed through the inside of the ferry, I spotted Harry and Rose. They both smiled at me and waved. I nodded my head and waved back. *Damn, I still haven't called Carroll to get Sara ready.* As I got in the car, I dialed Carroll's number.

Carroll answered, "Hello."

"Carroll, its Joe."

"Oh, hi Joey. How's everything? How's Brooke doing?"

"Not good Sis. I need you to get Sara ready for me. I just got off the ferry in Bremerton. I should be at your house in twenty, twenty-five minutes."

"Why Joey, what's wrong?"

"Two days ago she said she needs to see Sara, she… she… feels…" I couldn't bring myself to say it. "The hospital okayed it for Sara to come."

"Oh," was all Carroll could say, her voice trembling like she was about to cry.

"So can you, Sis, have her ready for me?"

"Yes, we both will be ready."

"Thanks Sis. I'll be there shortly." As I drove through Bremerton on my way to Belfair, I remembered Brooke loving it here. She said it was very similar to Montana—a lot of trees and mountain views. The only difference was that we were surrounded by the waters of the Sound, which she loved. Belfair was a small town—the complete opposite of downtown Seattle. We enjoyed the peacefulness of this little town. We would go for long walks by the lake, talking about anything that came to mind. She would always tease me about baptizing me in the lake. I smiled as I drove by the lake, remembering how I picked her up and jumped in the lake yelling, "Baptize this!" She screamed as we both went under. We came out of the water staring at each other and smiling. I remember the sun glistening off the water and reflecting on her face; she looked like an angel. I remember thinking how lucky I was to have found her. She smiled at me, moving the wet strands of hair from her face. Brooke swam over to me and wrapped her arms around my neck.

"Do you love me?" She just stared at me with those green eyes; there was an intensity in them that burned into my soul.

"With all my heart," I whispered.

"Is that all?" She said teasingly. I laughed out loud, then looked at her with the same intensity. I slowly helped her move a few more strands of wet hair. She stood still as I did this. I slowly slid my fingers down her cheek and rested them on her chin. She smiled contently, pushed away from me laughing, and added, "Good." As she swam back to the bank of the lake, I chased her, turned her around, and kissed her. She squirmed a little at first, still playing, but then gave in to my kiss and embrace. *What a great memory*, I thought as I pulled into Carroll's driveway.

I saw the curtain move indicating that someone was peeking outside. I got out of the car as Carroll opened the door and said, "We're ready."

"Hey, Sis. Give me a chance to use the restroom and we will head out. How's Sara?"

"She's fine. She's been sleeping a lot lately. I was thinking about taking her to the doctor."

"Maybe she just misses Brooke."

Carroll looked at me concerned. "Maybe," she replied. I went to the restroom and threw warm water on my face to try and thaw it out after the ride on the outside deck of the ferry. I looked around for a razor; I promised Brooke I would shave.

"Carroll," I called out.

"Yes?"

"Do you have a razor?"

"Yeah, upstairs in the master bath. I'll go grab it." She came back and knocked on the door. I half opened it and she passed me the razor. I just rubbed soap on my face; I didn't bother asking for shaving cream. Looking at myself, I noticed the deep, dark bags under my eyes. Here I was, thirty-two years old, and I looked more like forty-five. I finished up, wiped my face with a towel, and was ready to go. When I came out of the bathroom, Carroll was waiting with Sara in her basinet. I looked at Carroll and realized that all of this had taken a toll on her as well. She's been the one looking after Sara all these months while Brooke has been in the hospital. And I've just been popping in and out; she herself looked drained. I walked over and looked down at Sara. She stared back solemnly with the same green eyes as her mother's. I reached down, unbuttoned the straps, picked her up, and just held her. This peaceful, warm feeling ran through me. I kissed her on her forehead and strapped her back in.

I looked at Carroll. "Ready?"

She smiled a sad smile and said, "Ready." As I hit the highway, I was thinking, *Sara's already ten months old; she's about to be one.* I clenched the steering wheel at the thought of her first birthday without Brooke. *Damn, why?* I thought, *why?* I turned my thoughts to God again. I've just gone through the motions of church and her Bible study group all these years to keep Brooke happy. She always told me that she was worried about my soul because my faith was weak. I thought, *God if you're out there, don't punish Brooke. All she does is praise you, and she reads her Bible daily. Not only that, but what about Sara? Why punish a baby? Just take it out on me; I'm the one who doesn't believe.* Then I thought angrily, *this is just going into thin air, what's the point?*

I looked in the rear view mirror at Sara in the back seat, all strapped in. I remembered how happy we were when we found out

Brooke was pregnant. When we found out it was going to be a baby girl, we went shopping for all the cutest baby clothes. Everything was pink; I even got her a baby pink Seahawks jersey. I remember looking at Brooke as she would hold her belly lovingly. She would always say, "A gift from God." And I would jokingly respond, "Hey, I had a little something to do with it." She would just smile. Then, in her eighth month, during a checkup, they found a lump on her breast. They first thought that it was just a built up milk deposit, getting ready for her to nurse the baby. They said it happened sometimes. But, that wasn't the case. They applied a local anesthetic on the area of her breast with the lump. They did a biopsy and sent it for testing; it came back malignant. They couldn't give Brooke any treatment or operate to remove the tumor because of the baby. They said they could try some form of operation, but that there may be risks to the baby. Brooke refused and said, "We have a month to go; we will get to the operation and treatment after the baby is born."

I remember asking her, "Are you sure Brooke? This sounds serious." She looked at me with that fire in her eyes, and I knew there was no changing her mind. The day Sara was born it was pouring down rain. We rushed to the hospital after Brooke's water broke. She wasn't scared or nervous; she actually seemed excited. She said she couldn't wait to meet our little lady.

I was like, "Little lady? That sounds awkward."

"No, no its not," Brooke said, "she's going to be our little lady." I just smiled as I drove as safely and quickly as I could to the hospital. My windshield wipers sucked; I could barely see the road. Once we arrived at the hospital, I helped Brooke out of the car. I thought, *I've got to get those windshield wipers changed.* We rushed in through the hospital doors. Brooke had started to breathe heavily. I told the nurse that we were having a baby and asked if we could get her doctor here and her in a bed please. The nurse calmly looked at me.

"Sir, let me just finish up with this person in front of you, and I'll be right with you." I didn't even realize there was someone in front of me when I approached the nurses' station.

I looked at the guy in front of me and said, "Sorry bro, but my wife's about to give birth." He looked at me, then Brooke. She just smiled apologetically as she cradled her stomach.

The guy looked at the nurse and said, "Go head and help them first." He stepped aside. The nurse wasn't real happy with my insistent attitude, but I didn't care.

"Well I guess. What's your wife's name?" the nurse asked.

"Brooke Connelly."

"Date of birth?"

"August 11, 1985."

"Age of patient?" *Are you kidding me? I told this lady that my wife's having a baby! What's with the twenty-one questions?* The nurse just stared at me and said, "It's policy sir."

I looked at her dumbfounded. Luckily, Brooke stepped in, "I'm twenty-nine, and I'm so sorry ma'am. My husband is just really nervous; it's our first baby, so we're both excited and nervous at the same time." She smiled at the nurse; the nurse even managed a smile back before giving me a dirty look and turning her head away from us.

"Sheryl, can you get this young lady in a wheel chair and take her to room 102?"

"Thank you," I said sternly to the nurse as I saw the other RN come around and roll my wife off. When I was about to follow, the nurse stopped me.

"Sir, please fill out these forms and return them. Thank you," she said sarcastically. I just laughed; I must have sounded a little bit insane—like, 'are you serious?' I grabbed the clipboard, filled out the paper work, gave it back to the lady at the nurses' station, and asked, "Am I done?" She grabbed the clipboard back from me and looked very slowly over the papers I had just filled out—like she was reading a contract before signing. I'm growling in my head, thinking, *this lady!* When she said everything seemed to be in order, I took off to room 102 before she could say anything else to hold me up. I walked in the room and Brooke was already connected to IVs and a heart monitor. She looked at me as I came in the room; she reached out for me to come to her side. In two steps I was holding her hand. She smiled as she looked at me.

"How do you feel?" I asked.

"Excited, scared, happy."

"Wow, that's a lot of emotion you got going on there."

"Well, I don't get to do this every day you know," she said, giving me a slight punch on my shoulder. Then, she asked me how I felt. I was scared to death, but I had to be strong for her.

"I'm good. I just want everything to go as planned, so I can have you and the baby safely at home as soon as possible." She smiled. The doctor walked in the room and asked the nurse where we were. She told the doctor, "Nine centimeters." He looked at Brooke and I, smiling as he slid on white plastic gloves and said, "You guys ready to get this baby out of there?" Brooke grinned at his comment; I gave a half smile. I didn't think the doc's joke was funny, but yeah I was ready to meet my daughter. The doctor sat down facing Brooke. I was holding her hand and she was squeezing with immense strength; my hand was actually in pain from her squeezing so hard.

She was breathing heavily—somewhat panting in short breaths, while the doctor was coaching her through, "Almost there Mrs. Connelly; you're doing great." She was sweating profusely. I held her hand with one hand and caressed her head with the other.

"You're doing so good. I love you so much. You're almost done Brooke." I whispered to her. She would look at me, but not say anything. She wore a look of extreme concentration mixed with pain. I was dying inside to see her in pain like this. Then, I felt the pressure of her squeezing my hand relax and she laid her head back and let out a deep breath. Suddenly, I heard a cry. I turned my attention away from Brooke and there stood the doctor holding this tiny beautiful baby. *I'm a father, I'm a father!* That's all my mind kept repeating. I looked at Brooke in awe. "You did it beautiful, you did it." She smiled, exhausted.

They cleaned up our daughter and wrapped her up like one of those Mexican burritos before they brought her to Brooke. I hovered over them both with my right arm around Brooke and my left arm intertwined with Brooke's as we held our daughter together. We just stared at her, never saying a word—no words could describe the depth of our feelings at this moment. We both knew we couldn't love anything more in the world, and we never would. We were lost to this tiny little girl, who we named Sara after Brooke's mother.

Carroll and Richard were in the waiting room. I asked the nurse if she could go get them. Carroll busted into the room, tears streaming down her face. "Where's my niece? Where's my baby girl?" Brooke smiled and asked if Carroll wanted to hold her. Carroll squealed with delight, "Can I? Can I?" That's when I jumped in, "Be careful Carroll, don't drop my daughter?"

She made a face at me and said, "Shut up Joey, I would never." Carroll held Sara while Richard made baby noises at her. I bent over, kissed Brooke on the forehead, and told her that she has never looked more beautiful. She smiled, "Liar, but after what I just went through, I'll take it."

Sara was able to come home two days after her birth. They did some tests on Sara because of Brooke's condition while she was pregnant. They gave Sara a clean bill of health. Three weeks later, I had to sit in the hospital again waiting for Brooke to come out of surgery. They were removing the tumor, and were going to run other tests to see if the cancer was just localized to the tumor, or 'stage 1' as they called it. The doctor sounded pretty confident that Brooke seemed in good health and hinted that it would most likely be localized. So, by removing the tumor, we should be rid of the cancer. "I'm sure the other tests will come back negative," the doctor had said.

One week later, we were called in to see the doctor. He called Brooke himself around six in the evening; it seemed a little strange that the doctor would be calling that late for an appointment. He asked Brooke if she could be at the hospital at 9:00 am to discuss the results. Brooke held Sara that night looking at her lovingly; she was upset that she couldn't nurse Sara herself until she got the results back from the tumor removal and other tissue samples. We had to feed Sara baby formula. I could tell that Brooke was nervous and so was I. She put Sara to bed, then grabbed her Bible. She got on her knees by the side of the bed and prayed, like she did most nights. I could hear a desperation in her whispered prayers tonight. I laid there, looking up at the ceiling, wondering what the doctor was going to say about the results. I kept wondering why he would call so late. I looked over at Brooke;

she had finished praying and was looking at me. She smiled and asked me what I was thinking about. I lied and said, "Nothing much, I'm just wondering how that job is going in Tacoma. After we leave the doctor's appointment tomorrow, I might drive over to the jobsite to check it out."

Brooke smiled, "Cool, I want to check out that new Christian book store they opened up on Brinkley Street." We kissed goodnight, both trying to ignore the fear we felt about tomorrow—not knowing what the doctor would tell us.

We sat in the waiting room, nervously chatting about my work and hers. She worked at the university she graduated from as a research assistant to Professor Charles Rasmussen. I have to say, I didn't care for the guy. I met him a few times at a luncheon or a cocktail benefit. He just rubbed me the wrong way. I caught him looking at Brooke a couple of times and it wasn't as a colleague. I'm a guy, I know the look of lust. I never said anything to Brooke because she really respected him, but she knew I didn't like him. We were in mid-conversation when the nurse came to let us know that the doctor would see us now. We grabbed each other's hands, held them tightly, and followed the nurse. We walked in his office. He sat behind the desk facing the window in deep thought. The nurse actually startled him when she said, "Doctor Gordon, Mr. and Mrs. Connolly are here." He stood up, shook our hands, and asked us to sit.

We sat in silence until he began to speak, "Well, Mrs. Connelly, the tumor test did confirm that it was malignant. The other issue is that the results of the breast tissue also show signs of cancer cells, which have spread beyond the milk ducts, into the glands in the tissue around both breasts. This is a form of invasive breast cancer." As he was saying this, the room began to spin. I could hear him explaining, but I wasn't registering anything he was saying. I went completely numb, like I was in a dream. I was there, but not there.

I snapped out of it when Brooke began to cry, "No, no." I held her.

"I'm sorry, but that's the only way I feel we can stop its progression," The doctor said. I was thinking, *did I miss something?*

"What Brooke?" I asked, confused. She looked up at me with tears streaming down her face.

"They're going to take my breast Joey." I grabbed her as she sobbed into my chest.

The doctor said, "I'll give you some privacy." Then, he left his office. I held her as tightly as I could, my eyes watering up. I just kept thinking that I had to be strong for her. I lifted her chin and looked at her as I wiped her tears.

"Brooke, I know this hurts. I know you're scared, but you're still going to be the most beautiful woman in the world to me, even without your breast. The most important thing is that you're healthy." She tried to smile through her tears, but just buried her head back into my chest, as I rocked her, holding her tightly. On our way out, they gave us instruction's on what she could eat the night before and scheduled her operation for three days later. They said the sooner the better. We drove to Carroll's house to pick up Sara. I wasn't sure if Brooke wanted to get out of the car. She was quiet the entire drive over, just staring out the window and tracing the rain drops as they disappeared off the side of the window. When we arrived, she got out without a word.

We walked in the front door. Carroll was holding Sara, sitting at the small breakfast table in the corner of her dining room. She took one look at Brooke and I and her eyes watered as her lips began to tremble. I grabbed Sara from her arms as she walked over to Brooke; they just hugged each other. I stood there, glad that Brooke had my sister as I watched them hugging and crying. They went upstairs to Carroll's room to talk. I stood in the dining area holding my daughter. As I stared at Sara, I whispered to her, "We will get through this." I kissed her forehead.

When we got home that evening, Brooke sat out on the porch after feeding Sara and putting her to bed. She wasn't really saying much. She was in a state of shock after hearing that she was going to have to lose her breast in order to save her life. I watched her through the window, just sitting there staring out as the rain fell. I didn't know what to do, say, or how to act. I was at a complete loss. I walked in the kitchen, opened a bottle of wine, poured two glasses, and walked out to the porch. I sat down next to her and said, "Care for a glass of wine, beautiful?" She looked at me solemnly, accepted the glass, and took a sip. She surprised me by asking a question I didn't see coming.

"Joey, will you still want me after this operation? Will you look at me the same as you did before?" Tears started streaming down her face. I grabbed her glass and put it down. Wiping her tears, I held her close.

"You're my wife, my life, my everything. Nothing can or will ever change that." I pulled away and added with a smile, "Especially not two measly breasts." She gave me a slight smile.

"You say that now, but when I have the body of a little boy, what will you say then?"

I smiled and said, "You could never look like a little boy, even if you tried." Brooke managed a smile as she cried. I hugged her, took her face in my hands, and put two fingers on her chin. As I stared into her eyes, I repeated to her what I had whispered to Sara earlier, "We will get through this." I picked her up and carried her to our room and made love to her like we were the last two people on earth.

The following day was not a good day for Brooke. When I got home from checking on a few jobsites and stopping by the market for some groceries, I walked in yelling out, "I'm home." As I walked into the kitchen, I slowly put the bag of groceries down, taking in the scene and condition of our kitchen. There were broken dishes on the floor, and the toaster laid in the middle of the living room. I began calling out to her, "Brooke, Brooke!" I ran down the hall to the nursery and walked over to Sara's crib. She was sleeping peacefully. I watched as her chest rose and fell with each breath she took. Then, I ran across the hall to our room. I scanned the room; there was a broken lamp from Brooke's nightstand on the floor and a painting we had bought at a garage sale of a mountain range with two waterfalls—Brooke thought it was a peaceful piece of art—now hung sideways like it had been yanked, but it hung onto the wall by a thread. *Where is Brooke?* I thought I heard her voice come from the bathroom. I ran to the door and knocked. "Brooke, you alright?" She didn't say anything. "Brooke…"

"Leave me alone."

"Come on Brooke, open the door." I tried turning the knob, but it was locked.

"Leave me alone Joey, just leave me alone," she said again, and I could tell she had been crying. Then, I heard banging on the wall as she screamed, "Why God? Why?" I dropped to my knees outside that bathroom door as I heard her scream. It shook me to the very depths of my soul. She was screaming with every fiber of her being. I stood there, on my knees, my forehead leaning on the door as tears poured from my eyes. I realized there was nothing I could do to ease her pain and it killed me. I couldn't fix this; she depended on me and this was the one thing that I had no control over. I sat with my back against the bathroom door for the next hour. I didn't try to speak to her. I let her let it out of her system; it was mostly quiet now. I got up, walked to the kitchen, and opened the drawer where my dad kept all the spare keys to all the doors in the house. I went back to the room and tried five keys before I found the right one to the bathroom door. I slowly opened the door and stared at her for a second; she was sound asleep, curled up on the bathroom floor, holding her Bible close to her chest. I walked over to her, knelt down, and picked her up. I carried her to the bed, pushed the covers aside and tucked her in. Before I covered her, I tried to grab the Bible to put it aside. But she held onto it tightly, not wanting to let it go—holding it close to her chest. I sighed and covered her.

Five weeks later, Doctor Gordon had us in his office again explaining the different stages of breast cancer. I was tired and could only imagine how Brooke felt. It was exhausting being new parents and dealing with this fight for Brooke's life. But, we would never give up... never. As the doctor repeated his words, Brooke and I looked at him in disbelief, dazed from the last five weeks she was just starting to recover from. "Yes, um... um... as I was saying..." he could barely get the words out. He was trying to sound impartial, but I could tell the news he was giving us wasn't good. "Mrs. Connelly, it would appear your case has advanced beyond the breast area." He cleared his throat uneasily, "You have what is known as Stage four breast cancer, which means it has metastasized to other parts of your body." We just stared at him in complete shock, the room was quiet for just fifteen seconds, but it seemed like an hour before he continued, "Um… so there are many treatments we can start with. I will walk you—"

I cut him off mid-sentence, "Hold up Doc, you said that if we removed her breast it would stop the cancer from spreading. What the hell kind of place is this? My wife is cured, that's what you should be telling us. Now its metastic metas, well whatever you just said, we can't seem to get a straight answer from you. I… I…" Now, it was Brooke's turn to interrupt.

"Joey…" she touched my hand, she was trembling. I shut my mouth as I touched her hand, trying to hold it still. She asked the doctor questions and he walked us through different treatment options: hormone therapy, biological therapy—which involves a drug called Herceptin, which stops protein in HER2 from producing more cancer cells. Then, he stated that the most effective measure to date was chemotherapy.

He came around his desk sat in front of us and said, "I am truly sorry this is happening to you. We just didn't see this spreading so fast. You can discuss which treatment is best fitted to you. Take the day and let us know, and we will start scheduling your treatments."

Brooke looked up at the doctor, "It's not your fault." With tears streaming down her face, I saw that her comment had hit the doctor in the gut, but I wasn't feeling sorry for the guy. I thought there had to be something that he could have done better.

As I pulled into the hospital parking lot, it was drizzling lightly. I looked at Carroll and asked her if she brought something to wrap Sara in. She just nodded, and we got out of the car. As we walked in the front of the hospital, Carroll stopped as she held Sara. I turned to look at her, "What's wrong?"

"I don't know if I can see her like this. I haven't seen her in three weeks. How is she? Is... is she... or why is the hospital now letting Sara on the cancer ward floor." I saw that she was trembling, so I walked up to her and gently took Sara into my arms, nudging Carroll from her back and guiding her towards the elevators.

"She would really love to see you, Sis." Carroll loosened her shoulders like she was getting ready for a fight, giving herself the courage.

She nodded her head, "Let's go see my sister." I smiled at her as we walked into the elevator. We exited the elevators and walked by the waiting area. They had some service technicians pulling out the old coffee machine and installing a new one. I smirked at the machine thinking, *Good riddance.* We continued down the hall and Carroll noticed the nurses cleaning Jimmy's room. She stopped and looked at me, "Where's Jimmy?" I thought, *Damn I didn't tell Carroll that Jimmy passed on this morning.* I put my head down as I told her the news. Carroll looked at Jimmy's room, "That poor family. I only saw him a few times, but he was so full of life." I looked at my sister and gave her a light smile as I remembered Jimmy's freckled-face grin.

I was about to open the door to Brooke's room when Carroll paused, staring at the door. I looked at her; finally, she nodded at me as I opened the door. Brooke was wide awake; I guess anxiously waiting to see Sara. The nurses had put Brooke into a seated position. She sat there with her eyes staring intently at the door as we walked in. A huge smile came over Brooke's face as Carroll ran to her bed and gently hugged her. I walked over to the bed as Carroll stepped aside, wiping the tears from her eyes. Brooke stared in awe at Sara as I kneeled down so she could get a better look.

"She's gotten so big!"

"I know," I said. Sara stared at Brooke and squealed with a small laugh and a smile.

"Let me hold her."

I looked at Carroll, before saying, "Brooke, Sara is a heavy little girl and she moves a lot now." She gave me a sad look. "Oh alright, I will be near just in case she squirms out of your arms." I gently laid Sara in Brooke's arms. Brooke noticed the weight in her arms. As I saw her arms drop, I grabbed some pillows to prop under Brooke's arms to help support Sara's weight. Brooke looked up at me with smile, a 'thank you' for the help with the pillows. I stood there as Brooke and Sara stared at each other—their green eyes sparkling with love and a connection that only the two of them had. Sara sat so still, like she knew that her mother didn't have the strength to handle her usual kicking and squirming. She seemed so relaxed in Brooke's arms, just staring at her and making her baby noises—as if she had a lot to say to Brooke. I touched Brooke's shoulder as tears streamed down her face. She began telling Sara how much she loved her and how sorry she was that she wouldn't be there for her first date, her prom, for all the questions she would have as she became a young woman. Brooke looked at Carroll. Carroll was holding her hand to her heart as her eyes filled with tears. Brooke kept her eyes on Carroll.

"My beautiful baby girl, you will have God, your daddy, and for those womanly questions, I hope your Aunt Carroll will be there for those times to guide you in my place." Carroll let out a gasp as a water fall of tears broke through.

She came to Brooke's side, "I'll always be there for Sara, Brooke, always..." They looked at each other, then both looked at Sara as they cried. I stood there in silence, while my heart broke watching them; all I could do was have my hand on Brooke's shoulder and help her hold Sara. Suddenly, I felt Brooke's body jerk as she fought back a cough. She looked at me, her eyes wide open, and I knew she was about to have an attack, but she held it with all her might because she was holding Sara.

"Carroll, grab Sara now!" I ordered.

Carroll jumped, "What's happening?"

"Just get Sara." Carroll grabbed Sara and moved away from the bed. I held Brooke firmly as she grabbed my arm, her body convulsing as she coughed up blood. Carroll cried and offered to get a nurse.

"No, there's nothing they can do. Just take Sara out of the room." I held my wife as she got through the episode. When it was over, she looked exhausted. As I cleaned Brooke, I caught Carroll peeking in the door. When I was done, I told Carroll she could come in. She came in trembling as she held Sara, looking at me and then Brooke. It just hit me, Carroll had never seen Brooke go through one of her attacks.

It shook her up pretty bad. Brooke laid there very still with her eyes closed as she usually did after one of these episodes. I told Carroll, "I think I should get you guys home now."

"No, bring Sara. I want to see Sara," Brooke whispered.

"No Brooke, you're exhausted. You can barely speak."

"Bring her," she insisted. Even standing right next to her, I could barely hear her. I sighed and looked at Carroll; she had a dazed look on her face like she didn't know what to do. I took Sara in my arms; she was crying.

I patted her on the back and whispered, "Don't cry my sweet Sara." And I rocked her. I walked over to Brooke and knelt down so Brooke could see her. She just stared at Sara as Sara let out light whimpers and slowly stopped crying. Brooke put her fingers to her own lips, kissed them, and reached out to touch Sara on the forehead. She kept her hand there and I could tell that Brooke was praying as she whispered things I couldn't hear with her eyes closed, still holding her hand to Sara's forehead. When she was done, she folded her hands back on her chest and smiled. She watched me holding our daughter.

"Joey it's going to be you and Sara against the world. I love you both so much. Never forget to have her say her prayers." As she said this, tears rolled down her cheeks.

I whispered, "I will beautiful, don't cry." Her breathing was deep and slow. "Brooke…are you alright?" She nodded smiling.

"Always love her Joey," she said.

"Who?"

"Sara," she answered. I was thrown off by her comment.

"Of course I will."

She tapped her Bible, "This is Sara's. You know, it was my mother's. I want her to have it."

"Of course, honey. Brooke, you alright?" I asked again, she seemed off and wasn't making any sense.

She looked at me and Sara, smiled, then said, "God blessed me. God blessed me. I always asked him for a family of my own and here you are," she said, "Mom, what do you think?"

"Brooke, what are you talking about?"

Carroll came up behind me, "Brooke honey, what are you talking about?"

Brooke looked at Carroll and replied, "Jesus is letting my mom take me home." I gave Sara to Carroll.

"What are you talking about Brooke? Your mother's not here."

She looked back at me, "I'm sorry, Joey. I'm sorry, Joey."

"What? Brooke, what are... what's wrong?" I took her face in my hands.

She just smiled and said, "I love you so much." She touched my chin with two fingers. I held her hand against my chin.

"Brooke..."

"She is, I know Mom," Brooke whispered. I told Carroll go get a nurse now.

"She is what Brooke?" I asked.

"My mom said Sara's beautiful. Jimmy? Jimmy yes, butterflies, butterflies yes."

I was getting exasperated, my tone was curt, "Brooke what are you saying? Jimmy passed away this morning." I looked around the room. "What butterflies?" She looked at me.

"Jimmy's with them. He told my mom I was right."

I said, "With who?" Her breathing was so faint that it was almost like she wasn't breathing at all. I looked at her heart monitor—the beep was lessening, almost going flat. "Brooke, I love you. Don't go, not yet. I can't lose you, not yet, please."

She smiled and whispered, "You'll be fine. He's always there. Even when you think you're alone, He's there.

I just kept saying, "I love you, I love you." I held her hand to my chin as her eyes closed.

Still smiling, she said, "Love... love." Her chest rose and fell and did not rise again.

I yelled her name, "Brooke! Brooke!" The monitors started going off and I could hear Carroll crying in the background. It all seemed so far away as the nurses ran in to see what was going on with Brooke. One tried to move me out of the way, but I didn't budge. I just stood there holding her two fingers on my chin as I put mine to hers; I could barely even see her through my tears. There was a part of me that felt glad she wasn't in pain anymore, but the pain in my chest from losing her hurt so deep. I stared at my beautiful wife, who fought with every fiber of her being to live. I whispered, "I love you Brooke. I love you so much. I'll take care of our baby girl, don't worry." As I'm talking to my wife, the doctor touches me on my shoulder and says the words that will haunt me forever, "I'm sorry Mr. Connelly, but she's gone."

CHAPTER 4

Saying Goodbye

IT HAD BEEN FIVE DAYS since I lost Brooke, and they all felt like a blur. Her family from Montana flew in to SeaTac airport. I asked if I could pick them up but, Grandpa Frank refused and said, "Joe, you have plenty of other things to worry about besides picking up a bunch of mountain people." That made me smile. They stayed at a hotel in Bremerton called the Oyster Bay Inn. Every day since Brooke's passing, there have been lots of friends, neighbors, and people from church coming by and calling to give their condolences. It just all seemed hazy to me. I remember going through the motions—more like a robot than anything. It hasn't even settled in yet that Brooke is gone. Just yesterday, I was brushing my teeth and her tooth brush was still sitting in the tooth brush holder. I almost expected her to be in right behind me, telling me to get out of the way. "It's my turn!" she would say as she nudged me in the ribs to let her get a corner of the sink and mirror. I just couldn't seem to acknowledge that I won't ever see her again, talk to her, hear her voice, feel her touch. It doesn't seem possible.

Carroll was a huge help in scheduling everything—where the services were going to be held, dealing with the caterers, the florist, and all of the other details.... not to mention helping me with Sara. There was the question of where Brooke would be buried. Her family mentioned that they had a plot in Montana next to her mother, but I told them that I wanted to keep her close. They said they understood and never mentioned it again.

I woke up this morning at 3:30 and was unable to go back to sleep. I was remembering the last words I shared with my wife. She wasn't making any sense—talking about her mom, Jimmy, and apologizing to me. For what? My mind raced. Brooke stood so strong and waited until she got to hold Sara one last time before she left. I frequently wonder if this ache in my heart will ever go away. What really baffles me is that Brooke and Jimmy passed away on the same day.

I got up, threw on some sweats, and grabbed my iPod before I went outside to stretch. It was chilly this morning, but I enjoy the cold. I turned on the iPod and started scrolling through my playlists when I ran into Brooke's playlist. I smiled, remembering how I used to tease her about taking over everything she got her hands on. She had her own iPod, but reasoned that she would have to put all of her playlists on mine just in case she lost hers or forgot it at the house. I opened her playlist; it had mostly Christian music in it. She had bands like Building 429, Falling Up, and Abandon. Brooke would always listen to Abandon. I pressed play on a song called 'Feel it in Your Heart' and the melody came blasting into my ears.

As I hit the road running. I thought about how Brooke dedicated a lot of time to God—Jesus. I would go to church with her and go through the motions, just to keep her happy, but I've never been sure about any of it. Hearing her music now makes me feel like she's near. It was Christian rock, of course, but the music was actually good. As I ran, I contemplated my life without Brooke—raising Sara, living day to day. Brooke made me promise to raise Sara with prayer and to keep God in our home. How am I supposed to teach my daughter something that I'm not sure I believe in? But, I made a promise to my wife while she laid on her death bed.

Before I knew it, I was six miles from the house. All of these thoughts had me so distracted that I hadn't even realized how far I'd gone. I guess I was just trying to run out all of this built up frustration.

It was almost as if I was running away from the reality of losing Brooke. I stopped running and bent over to catch my breath. I looked up after a few seconds and noticed that I was three blocks from Brooke's church; the one where her services were going to be held. She spent so much time here volunteering, that they were more than glad to host Brooke's services. I walked the three blocks to the church. It was about 5:30 am and the sun was just starting to peek over the mountains. I stood directly in front of the church and took the ear phones out of my ears. I just stared, conflicted about how much belief and love she gave to Jesus, and how little of that I was able to give.

The sun had started to touch the tip of the church; it was a beautiful building. Like my dad, I've grown to appreciate well-built structures. Hell, I was going to be an architect. It was a large white building with two large pillars in the front and a castle-like tower above, hollowed out with the shape of a cross. When the sun shone through it, the shadow cast on the back wall of the church almost took on the form of a flaming cross. Brooke loved the time of the day when she was able to see it like that. I stood here with the urge to talk, but then I thought, *who the heck I am going to talk to?* I looked up at the hollowed cross, and I just started talking... I guess to God.

"So... God is it, or do you prefer Jesus? Well anyway, I'm standing here in front of your church—you have many of them I guess—this one isn't the largest, more like a town home." I thought, *what the heck am I doing? I'm talking to a building for God-sake.* Yet, I continued, "Well I guess my question is... my wife, Brooke, she loved you even when all the bad things in life happened—like earthquakes that killed hundreds of people, or when some man murdered an entire family. She always said, 'We don't know why these things happen. Sometimes you just have to have faith and believe that God has His plan. All we can do is pray and believe'. Well, God, why did you take my wife? She served in your church and prayed every day. We just had a beautiful baby girl, and you took her. Can you explain that? I'm waiting, Almighty God! What's the matter..."

Suddenly, I was cut off by a voice, "What the heck is all the noise about?" I looked around a little startled. For a split second, I thought God was speaking back to me. Then, I saw some newspapers ruffle and move on the side of the church, behind one of the pillars. A man sat up and said, "Young man, what seems to be the trouble? Who are you arguing with? The church people don't usually show up until 9:00 am."

"I'm sorry to wake you I... I... was just praying," I lied. I knew this man. He was a homeless, older, black man—I would guess in his late sixties. He showed up for Sunday service many times. Some of the other church goers complained to the pastor about him attending, but the pastor always replied, "This is God's house, and all of His children are welcome." So, some of those people chose a different church. Brooke used to bring him bagels and give him money when she saw him. She told me that's what she loved about this church. "It's what God would want—no judgment, just come as you are", she would say.

The homeless man replied, "Man, what does it take to get a good night's sleep around here? I left the city to come down here to this nice, white, suburban town, and I still can't get no rest. Gosh danget. So you says you was praying? Well it sounded more like arguing to me, with some sarcasm. Well as long as you're talking to God, that's all that matters. Go on son, have your spat with God, just do me a favor... try to keep your voice down. I was in the middle of a great dream; I was on a beach in Hawaii with a beautiful woman."

"Sorry, sir, I was on my way," I said.

"Suit yourself," he replied as he patted something that resembled a pillow and laid his head back down. I headed back down the road home—this time in silence. It was nice to enjoy the sounds of the morning. I strolled back to the house still thinking about Brooke and how much I missed her. There was a part of me that wished all of her pain would just be over, but not having her here with me hurts so much more. I would give anything just to make her smile again, to hear her voice. I spontaneously laughed out loud thinking, *she's actually rubbed off on me after all these years.* I even tried talking to God at five-thirty in the morning standing in front of a church. I felt like an idiot.

I don't know if I'm ready for this day—for all of the people coming to say goodbye to my wife. I'm not ready to say goodbye. I'm not sure if I can deal with all of the 'I'm so sorry for your loss' comments. I hated it when I lost my parents, and I know I'll hate it now with my wife. I guess I just have to put on a show and be as strong as I can—when in reality I'm scared. I don't know how to live without Brooke. She was my life. And Sara... how do I raise her without Brooke? I can't fathom doing it without her. All of these thoughts won't stop swirling around in my mind. How am I going to get through today? Today, I bury my wife.

When I got home, Carroll was already up and on the phone making arrangements—calling the florist to make sure everything was good to go. I looked at her on the phone and thought, *what would I do without my sis.* I walked down the hall to my room. On the way, I stopped and looked into Sara's nursery. She laid in her crib asleep. I gently touched her cheek, thinking about how much I love this little girl. I smiled as I laid my two fingers on her chin, remembering my wife. My poor daughter will grow up never knowing how wonderful her mother was. Sara has always been so calm; she really doesn't cry much and she sleeps a lot. Which was surprising because I heard that babies keep you up all night. Well, I thought she was the best.

I finished the walk to my room and pulled out my suit from the closet. *I guess I've got to get ready for today.* I wish I could just fast forward through today, so that I didn't have to deal with it. But, I know there is no way around it. I laid out my suit on the bed and jumped in the shower. When I was done, Brooke's family was already in the house helping Carroll set up for the reception after the service—so family and friends could come over to celebrate Brooke's life. I really wasn't thrilled about the idea, but Carroll insisted that it was important to have a get-together—not just to mourn, but to give people closure and talk about how wonderful Brooke was. I put on my clothes, then attempted my tie. I always had problems with this part, and Brooke was always the one to help me. She would slowly walk me through each step, loop by loop. I finally gave up messing with the tie, sat on the bed, and cried. After a few minutes, I shook it off and headed downstairs after doing the best I could with the tie. Grandpa Frank was setting up chairs along with Will and Dan, Brooke's cousins. I walked over and started helping when Frank said, "Relax Joe, we got it."

I smiled, "I gotta stay busy or I'll lose my mind."

"I understand," Frank said returning my heartbroken smile. Brooke's grandmother, Kathryn, walked in just then and came over to me.

"How are you honey?" she asked, giving me a big hug with tears in her eyes. "I can only imagine how you feel. How's Sara? Is she sleeping?"

"Yeah, last I checked, she was sound asleep in her crib."

"That little girl sure does sleep a lot…even for a baby. I have to get her up and ready," Carroll added as she headed down the hall to Sara's nursery.

Grandma Kathryn looked at me again, "Son, your tie is a mess." I smiled again, looking down at the embarrassment around my neck.

"Yeah I know, Brooke used to always be the one to help me with it." I just stood quietly, swallowing another knot of emotion gathering in my throat. I didn't want to break down in front of her family.

Grandma Kathryn looked at me with terribly sad eyes, "Don't worry about it; I'll take care of it for you. Who do you think did those three ties this morning?" Frank, Dan, and Will all looked at her wryly.

"Yes my darling, where would I be without you?" Frank said. She just smiled, satisfied with his response as she fixed my tie. She patted me on the shoulders and said, "There, you look like a million bucks now." I smiled down at the tie.

"Thanks, it looks great," I said.

The time came for us to pack into the cars and head to the church. Once we arrived, Phil was standing out front smoking a cigarette. I kept telling him to quit, but he always just said, "Sorry Joey, old habits die hard." Then, I would always reply, "Or they kill you." He would laugh and respond, "We all gotta go sometime." I walked over to him. He put out the cigarette, put his hands on my shoulders, and asked how I was doing.

I looked at him and shrugged my shoulders, "As good as I can be I guess."

"Son, every day is a new step forward... just remember that. I'll go see what your sister needs help with," he said, patting my shoulder. I nodded my head, watching as he walked over to Carroll.

Little by little, friends, family, and acquaintances started filtering in. Before I knew it, all of the church's seating was full. It almost looked as if there was a full service going on. Carroll had me standing at the entrance of the church with her while Grandma Kathryn watched Sara. I asked Carroll if it was absolutely necessary.

She just looked at me and said, "Joey, I know how hard this is for you, and I know you don't want to be around people right now, but it is customary for the immediate family to greet friends and family who are coming to say goodbye to Brooke. I love you Joey, and I know your dying inside, but you have to do this."

I nodded my head, "Alright Sis, and thanks by the way… for everything you've done—setting all this up. I really think it's beautiful. Brooke would have loved the decorations. I love you, Sis. I don't know what I would have done without you. She gave me a big smile and hugged me.

"You're my brother and Brooke's my sister," she said with tears in her eyes. As Carroll took her place opposite me, Professor Charles Rasmussen walked up. He began saying how sorry he was for my loss, and I felt my stomach turn. I couldn't put my finger on it, but this guy just rubbed me the wrong way.

I faked a smile and said, "Thanks for coming Professor."

He then turned to Carroll and said, "You are?" He stood with his hand out, waiting for her to take it. I was surprised when Carroll didn't shake it. A look of disgust was written all over her face, which shocked me.

"I'm Joey's sister," she responded, "Excuse me, I have to see the pastor about something." Then, she abruptly walked away. I stood there amazed by her mannerisms. Just a few moments ago, she had asked me to have the courtesy to stand here and greet people coming to say goodbye.

Professor Rasmussen said, "Well, Mr. Connelly..." as he slowly turned his gaze away from Carroll walking away. "I truly am sorry about your loss. We all loved Brooke in our department. It was sad to see her go to another department in the university right before she got sick." I looked at him baffled; I don't remember Brooke telling me that she left Professor Rasmussen's department. He saw the surprised look on my face, but I quickly changed my expression.

"Well come in Professor. Please have a seat and thanks again for coming." As he walked away, I thought, *what is he talking about? I didn't know Brooke left his department, and what the heck got into Carroll? Why did she act the way she did with the Professor?* That's when I noticed a man just outside the door looking at the large picture of Brooke. I walked outside once I realized that it was the homeless man I woke up this morning in front of the church.

He looked up and said, "I'm sorry I don't mean to pry, I just remember this young lady. She was an angel. You know, she would always bring me a cup of coffee and a bagel in the mornings. At 9am, just like clockwork. When I didn't see her anymore, I asked the pastor what happened to her, and he told me that she was sick in the hospital with the cancer. It broke my heart to hear it; someone like her definitely didn't deserve to go through something like that. I prayed, you know, every day for this young lady, but God wanted this angel home." The old man took off this tattered, gray hat and put it over his heart. He looked at me again and recognition washed over his face, "Hold on, you're this young lady's husband... I remember seeing you on Sundays with her at service. She talked about you all the time... Joey right?"

"Yeah. Well, Joe actually."

"My sincerest condolences Joey. By the way, I'm Billy... Billy Jones," he said extending his hand.

"Thanks Billy," I said taking his hand and smiling at the fact that he still called me 'Joey'. Carroll walked up and told me that the services were about to start. When Billy started walking back down the steps of the church, I asked him where he was going.

He said, "I wouldn't want to intrude on you and your family."

I said, "No Billy, I truly believe Brooke would've wanted you here." He smiled up at me and came inside, sitting down in the back row. The pastor spoke about Brooke and all of her good deeds—how she was a loving wife, mother, and daughter, and what she meant to others. As he said all of this, I sat there hearing him, but feeling so distant, as if this still wasn't really happening. I stared at the coffin that held my wife's body—my beautiful Brooke. It just didn't seem possible.

Then, I realized that Carroll was shaking my arm saying, "Joey... Joey." I snapped out of my daze and looked at her. "The pastor asked you to say a few words about Brooke." I realized that everyone was staring at me. As I looked around, all I saw were saddened eyes, mostly filled with pity. Then I looked up, passed the coffin, and saw the pastor gesturing for me to come up. *Damn, I forgot. He did mention the night before that he was going to have me say a few words to family and friends.* I stood up, feeling anxious. My palms were sweaty, and I really didn't know what to say. Should I speak the truth about how angry I am, how I don't want to accept this? All I've heard from people lately is 'trust in God, its Gods Plan'. Well, I'm tired of it! What kind of God plans to take someone's wife? Someone who just had a beautiful baby girl who will never meet the wonderful person her mother was—never hear her voice, her laughter. How do I give that back to Sara?

My hands were clenched into fists as I reached the altar. I stood there, seeing all the same looks of sadness and pity. I grabbed the corners of the podium and, looking down, I began laughing. I don't know why I started laughing, but I couldn't stop. Everyone just stared at me. Once I was able to get ahold of myself, I began. "Well… here we all are to say goodbye to Brooke. What can I say, I'm not ready to say goodbye," I said, looking down at her coffin. Carroll stood up and slowly began walking towards me. I stopped her in her tracks, "No Carroll, I'm fine. I have a few things I want to say. You know, my wife was probably one of the sincerest people I've ever met in my life. She always considered others, even when she was sick herself. She always put others first. Now, I have to ask myself this one question… why? Why?" I began laughing again; then, my laughing turned into something like hysterical crying as I continued, "Why? Can someone tell me why? How about you Pastor Mike, you tell me, since all you keep telling me is its Gods plan. Tell me why… no you know what, better yet, tell my daughter why her mother's no longer here because God chose to take her. What do you think she will say to that when she's five, huh? Tell me." My eyes were filled with tears.

I didn't notice someone standing at my side; it was Phil, grabbing me by my arms saying, "Joe get ahold of yourself, don't do this. Now's not the time." Phil pulled me aside firmly. I looked and saw Billy Jones stepping up to the altar.

He cleared his throat and said, "Hello ya'll, I have a few words to say about this young lady if you don't mind." He looked at Pastor Mike for confirmation; the pastor nodded his head. "Well, as you know, I'm a homeless man and, looking around this church, I don't recognize all of you, but some faces are familiar. You would know me if you attended the Sunday services here because I sleep right outside this church. Most of the time people walk by me, ignore me like I'm not there, and I ain't never bothered no one neither. I don't ask for handouts or money," he stood up straight, feeling pride in what he was saying. "But this young lady here," he gestured toward Brooke's coffin, "always, and I mean *always,* took the time to smile at me, come over to say hi, and called me by my name… my name. Now, for most folks, that don't seem like much of nothin, but when you ain't got two dimes to rub together and all you got in this world is the clothes on your back, well… it means a whole lot. This person saw me; she actually saw me," he banged his chest as he said this. "And when you walk around day in and day out, people passing you by like you don't exist, or cross the street just to avoid walking on the same side as you, well you start to believe you ain't worth nothin. She made me feel like a person again." His eyes filled with tears as he looked around the church. "Now, I understand this young man is in a lot of pain—pain that none of us can feel at this moment—but I just want you to know," Billy looked right at me as he said this, "I know I don't look like much, and it might not mean much coming from someone like me, but your wife was something special son. She made me feel human again when I was starting to believe that I wasn't." Billy touched his heart. "She was a gift from God who touched my soul." He looked at everyone again. "Well, I've said my piece." Billy nodded at the pastor, stopped on his way down from the altar, kissed his fingers, and touched Brooke's coffin before he continued down the aisle and made his way out of the church.

CHAPTER 5

Getting to Know Sara

I WAS PRETTY MUCH IN cruise control mode from that point on. People would come by, touch my shoulder, and say 'sorry' again. I would smile and say 'thanks' and apologize again for my outburst at the altar. Everyone seemed to understand. My entire life crumbled as I watched Brooke's coffin being lowered into the ground. It had started to rain, and the pastor wrapped up the ceremony. People began walking to their cars.

It's time to go Joey," Carroll said, gently resting her hand on my forearm.

I just stared at her blankly, "I'm fine where I'm at."

"Well, I gotta get Sara home and out of this rain," she replied. I didn't look at her, my gaze was locked on Brooke's grave. I just nodded as she walked away. I stood there in the rain, watching the cemetery workers fill the grave with dirt. Before I knew it, I was alone and soaking wet, staring at Brooke's grave as the fresh pile of dirt turned to mud. I looked up and saw Phil sitting in his truck, watching me as he smoked a cigarette.

I looked back at Brooke's grave. "This hurts so much Brooke. I would give anything to have you back—even just one more day in the hospital, even through all the pain. I just want to talk to you, to tell you that I'm sorry for all the times I didn't pay attention to you or forgot something that was important to you. I don't know how to live life without you. I'm lost Brooke, I'm so lost." My tears blended with the rain as they slid down my face. I finally turned and walked toward Phil's truck, dreading going home to deal with everyone at the reception.

Phil pulled up to the house, and there were numerous cars parked in front. Phil pulled around the back, by the garage, and parked the truck. Then, he looked at me and said, "You gonna be alright kid?" I just looked at him with both hands on the dashboard. I couldn't speak—no words would come out; only tears filled my eyes. "Damn son..." He grabbed me, pulled me to his chest, and held me as I cried. I broke down completely. I cried like a child, asking 'why... why?' He just held me, telling me to let it out. "Let it out. I'm here for you, go head son." I was finally able to pull myself together and sat up.

"Sorry Phil," I said as I wiped the tears from my eyes.

"Don't be, I've been watching you Joey; you've been holding it in. You had to let it out. There's no shame in a man crying kid, especially after losing his wife." I looked at him, still sniffling a bit.

"Thanks Uncle Phil."

"You haven't called me that in years," he said with a laugh. Then, his face became very serious. "Joey, I'll always be your Uncle Phil, always son. You know that don't you?"

"I know, I know," I said, managing a smile. I looked at his shirt; it was all wet from where I cried when he held me. "Sorry about getting you all wet." He looked down and smiled.

"Don't worry about it kid." Then, he looked toward the house, "You ready?" I looked at him, wiped my eyes one last time, and nodded.

When we walked through the back door by the kitchen, Carroll was setting up what looked like mini corn dogs on a platter. Phil took it from her and walked into the living room, putting it in the center where guests could grab them as they pleased. Carroll looked at me and asked how I was doing.

"I'm alright. You need any help?"

"No, I'm good." Then, she grabbed my coat and touched my shirt. She looked at me with huge eyes. "Joey you're soaked. You need to jump in the shower and get into some dry clothes before you get sick."

"Alright mother," I said smiling. She smiled back.

"Make it quick, we have guests." I headed down the hall to my room. A few minutes later, I threw on some jeans and was about to throw on a T shirt when I thought about Carroll complaining about that. So, instead, I looked in the closet and found a decent light-blue button up shirt. I headed toward the door. With my hand on the knob, I took a deep breath, opened the door, and headed down the hall to greet our guests. When I walked in, everyone grew quiet. I stood there for a second, wondering what to say, when Grandpa Frank walked up and said, "Joe I have a few questions about those nice, sturdy, wooden tool cupboards out in the garage."

I smiled at him, "My dad built those years ago." I was thankful for Grandpa Frank; he was like a life vest that saved the moment for me and everyone continued with their conversations. I began to walk the room, thanking some of Brooke's friends from college for coming. A few of her friends from Bible study thanked me for having them and told me how much they loved her—then they invited me to their Bible study. I smiled and said, "Yeah maybe." As I shook their hands, I looked up and saw Phil and Grandpa Frank talking. Phil looked back at me and winked. Grandma Kathryn was holding Sara. I had a sudden urge to hold my daughter.

I walked over to Grandma Kathryn and asked, "Do you mind me taking this young lady off your hands for a bit?" She smiled and handed Sara over. As I held Sara, she just stared at me with those dazzling green eyes. I put two fingers on her chin and she smiled and goo-ed at me, trying to grab my fingers with her little chubby hand and nibble on them. *I love her so much*, I thought as I looked at her in wonder. Brooke and I created this beautiful little girl. As I looked at her, all I could think was that I had to be strong for her. *I have to raise her on my own now.* That thought scared the heck out of me. Carroll walked over to me and said that it was time to feed Sara and put her to bed. I told her that I would take care of it. She looked at me and noticed that some of the guests were leaving.

"I got this. You see everyone out and don't forget to thank them for coming."

"Seriously Carroll?"

"Yes, you barely spent any time with anyone."

"Alright Sis." I stood at the door as everyone started to leave, all saying 'thanks' and telling me not to hesitate to call if I needed anything. I shook hands and said 'thanks' until almost everyone was gone. I turned around and found Frank, Kathryn, and their nephews cleaning up. Phil folded up the table and took it back to the garage. I followed him and asked how work was going. I told him that I would be back tomorrow.

"There's no rush, I got it."

"I gotta do something, Phil, or I'll go crazy."

"It's up to you kid."

"Thanks Phil. Well, I'll see you then." After he drove off, I headed back into the house. Grandpa Frank and Grandma Kathryn were all wrapped up and ready to leave. They both hugged me and reminded me to call if I needed them. Kathryn touched my cheek and said, "You'll get through this, Joey. I know it's hard. I remember when I lost my Sara, Brooke's mother." Her eyes watered at the mention of her name. "You've got to stay strong, especially for the little one." I touched the hand she had placed on my cheek.

"I will," I assured her. I shook Brooke's cousins' hands as they said goodbye. I was still standing there, watching them drive off, when

Carroll came up behind me with two beers and said, "Care for one?" I smiled and replied, "Yes, definitely. Thanks." Carroll took a seat on the porch bench and began to ask how I was when I stopped her. "Sis, I love you, but I don't think I can take one more 'how are you doing'."

"I'm sorry," she nodded in understanding, "I'm just worried about you."

"I'll be fine." She looked at me as I said this. She knew me too well. I shrugged and looked away. "Well hell, I don't know Carroll. I just lost my wife, I have a baby to take care of, and well… I don't know what's next I guess."

"Don't worry Joey, you're a great father. You'll make Brooke proud."

"I hope Sis, I hope," I said, taking another sip of my beer. We spent the rest of the night talking about Brooke, all the quirky stunts she used to pull, all the people she helped, and her laugh—she had the funniest laugh.

Carroll woke me up the next morning saying she was headed home— that Richard wanted to take her out for breakfast.

"Richard?" I questioned.

"Yeah, I'm thinking about giving him a second chance. He technically is still my husband you know."

"Alright Sis, good luck," I said stretching in my bed.

"Thanks. I checked on Sara; she's still sleeping. I have a bottle ready, all you have to do is heat it up. Luke warm." I sat up immediately, as the realization hit me that I've never taken care of Sara on my own before. Brooke or Carroll have always been around, and for the last six months, I basically lived in the hospital with Brooke.

I jumped out of bed, "Carroll hold on, I might need some help on what she eats after the bottle or when she needs a diaper change or…" Carroll broke out laughing.

"Joey she's just a baby. She will cry when she's hungry and you can check if she's wet or you'll smell when she needs a diaper change." She was out the door and in her car before I could stop her. I turned around and stared down the hall where Sara was sleeping. I suddenly had this fear of being alone with my daughter. *Carroll's right, she's just a baby. How hard can it be?* I laughed to myself.

I stopped by Sara's room to check on her. She was still fast asleep. I thought, *I'll shower then feed her the bottle.* As I poured the shampoo on my head and started scrubbing, I thought about how good and calm Sara is. I smiled thinking that I had the greatest baby in the world. It was at that moment that I heard a screeching scream that made me jump. I opened my eyes and got soap in them—it burned like hell. I reached for the curtain to pull it open so that I could get to Sara, but my eyes were burning and blurred, so I didn't see the soap on the bath tub floor. I stepped on it and slipped forward, yanking the shower curtain down, and hitting the left side of my eye on the knob as I fell. "Damn it!" I yelled as Sara still cried in the next room. I jumped up out of the tub, grabbed a towel to wipe my face and eyes with, then wrapped the towel around my waist and ran to Sara's room.

She was screaming so loud. I started to baby talk to her saying, "It's alright my little angel, Daddy's here." I picked her up and she started to calm down. I walked over to my room holding her with one arm as I went through my closet to grab a pair of jeans and a shirt. She seemed to have calmed down enough that I could put her in the middle of my bed without worrying about her. It was a King size bed, so I put her in the middle to keep her away from the edge. I went in to the restroom, washed my eyes out and dried off. I slid on my boxer briefs and walked out of the restroom. I immediately saw that Sara was about to roll off the bed. I slid on my knees and caught her just as she made her last turn that would have led her to a three-foot fall. I let out a sigh of relief as I held her. I looked at her and asked, "Where are you trying to go little girl?" She stared back, trying to answer me with a 'goo gaa goo' and smiling. I smiled back thinking, *I'm out of breath, half-blind with a knot growing on the left side of my eye, and I've only been alone with Sara for ten minutes. I guess I've got my work cut out for me.*

For the most part, the rest of the day went well—other than the throbbing pain I had on the left side of my eye. I fed Sara her last bottle for the evening and put her in her crib. She was slowly falling asleep, but I could tell she was fighting it. I began to whisper a song to her:

> *Baby hair with a woman's eyes, I can feel you watching*
> *In the night, all alone with me and we're waiting for the sunlight*
> *It's you and me forever.*
> *Sara smile. Mmmm...*

She closed her eyes and fell asleep. As I covered her with a blanket, I whispered thanks Hall and Oats, the group that wrote the song. I didn't realize how exhausted I was until I laid down on my bed. *I need to call Carroll tomorrow and figure out a babysitter so I can get back to work.* Phil called me today mentioning three prospective bids we had on three major builds; the investors wanted to sit with the owner to discuss schedule and costs. This was my last thought as I closed my eyes and fell into a dead asleep.

I was awakened by a loud ringing, which startled me for a moment, but then I remembered setting the alarm for 6:00 am. I pressed the snooze button and ten minutes later the frantic ringing continued.

"Alright already," I said as I turned off the alarm. I sat up in bed feeling somewhat rested. I haven't slept that long, or straight through that many hours, in a long time; it didn't feel normal. I got up and walked over to check on Sara. She was on her side with a slender stuffed monkey wrapped around her right arm. She looked so relaxed, but after yesterday, I didn't want to get caught in the shower again, so I started working up a game plan to get Sara relaxed and fed so that I would be in a good position to shower.

I walked to the kitchen and started putting a bottle together and warming up the milk. I grabbed the car seat and carried it over to my bed. I was ready for Sara this morning. I smiled to myself thinking that I had a handle on this. I picked Sara up and an unrelenting smell came from her diaper. I said, "Sara what did I feed you?" I know Carroll told me to give her smashed bananas yesterday, but wow! I was overwhelmed by the smell. I laid her on the bed and slowly began taking of her pajama suit. Her poop had come out of the diaper and was going up her back. She was giggling and goo-ing while I was over here gagging. I looked up at Brooke's picture and said, "Our daughter is killing my sense of smell beautiful, but I can do this Brooke." I grabbed tissue and stuffed both my nostrils so I could power through the smell. When I took off the diaper, it looked like a poop grenade had gone off. I began the treacherous job of cleaning her. I must have used a whole box of baby wipes. Sara just stared at me with her mother's green eyes and her tiny hands balled up into little fists; she was posed like she was a boxer ready to fight. She looked so cute, even after bombarding me with her poop.

Now, I gotta bathe her, I thought as I looked around. I knew there was a little tub in her room, but it seemed so far away, and I didn't want to leave her on the bed by herself—especially after the stunt she pulled yesterday. Then, I got a great idea. I carried her over to the bathroom sink, turned on the hot and cold water, and ran my hands under it until it was warm—not too hot and not too cold. Then, I sat her in the sink. The only soap available was the hand soap, so that's what I used. Sara was trying to grab the stream of water coming out of the faucet. She looked amazed every time she grabbed it and her little hand went right through. After washing her off, I wrapped her in a towel, carried her over to the bed, and made sure to tuck in the towel tightly around her—like a burrito, so that she couldn't move while I got her a change of clothes and a new diaper. I picked out this little outfit that said, 'I'm mommy's little angel'. I smiled as I thought about Brooke. Oh how I wished that she was here. I missed her so much. I headed back to my room and there was Sara sitting up with the towel unraveled at her side. She saw me coming and rolled to her right, as if to run off the bed. I grabbed her saying, "Sara you're always trying to escape, you crazy little girl." She definitely had Brooke's adventurous spirit.

I got her a new diaper, changed her, and buckled her in the car seat with a bottle. I sat down and said, "Whew...that took a bit of time." I looked at the clock, "I don't even really have time to shower now." I threw on my boots and looked at Sara. "Ready to go to work my angel?" She just stared at me while she drank her bottle. I smiled at her, picked up the car seat, and started for the door. I stopped in front of a large framed drawing of Brooke and I. I remembered having this drawing done; we were in Hawaii on vacation, walking down Waikiki Blvd. This artist was doing portraits, so we sat for him to do one of us. I complained the whole night that the drawing didn't look anything like me, but he did capture Brooke's eyes and her beauty. I stared at the drawing now, while I held the car seat with one hand. I ran my two fingers across Brooke's cheek and rested them on her chin, whispering, "I miss you my love... so much that I can't breathe." I was interrupted by a bang on the floor. I looked down, and Sara had dropped her bottle. I sighed, reached down to pick it up, and looked at the drawing one last time before we headed out.

It was a beautiful morning as we drove down the road. I looked in the rearview mirror, keeping an eye on Sara. She just stared out the window. I could only guess that she was mesmerized by the morning sun peeking through the trees as we drove by. I drove up to a drive through coffee stand; I was in dire need of some caffeine. There was a car in front of me. As I waited, I thought about Billy Jones and what he said about Brooke always taking time to stop and bring him a cup of coffee. I thought, *well the church is about a half mile from here. I'll honor*

Brooke and take him a cup of coffee. I smiled. Hearing Billy talk about Brooke at the service, I didn't realize how something as small as a cup of coffee could make someone feel. He said she saw him; I guess now, when I think about it, I'd never really noticed him all those years we went to church.

I didn't realize the car in front of me had gone until I looked up and saw the coffee girl waving her hands at me to drive up. When I reached the stand, the coffee girl asked what she could get for me.

"Two large vanilla lattes please," I said.

She smiled and said, "I'm on it." She came back with the two coffees, and when she handed me the holder she saw Sara and started to say how cute she was. She leaned half way through my window making baby noises at Sara. Sara just stared at her almost the same way I looked at this girl—like 'what are you doing?' Finally, the girl stood up and asked, "Where's mama? Or are we a cute single dad?" As she said this, she gave me this flirtatious grin. I was thinking, *seriously? Is this girl flirting with me with my daughter in the car?*

"What do I owe you?" was all I responded with, not even answering her question. She looked at me puzzled and said, "Three ninety-five." I gave her a five-dollar bill and drove off. I looked back at Sara and said,

"That's the last time we go to that coffee stand, huh beautiful?" Sara goo-ed, trying to answer as if she agreed with me. I smiled as I drove. I stopped in front of the church looking in the direction of the pillars where Billy slept, but I didn't see him. I looked around again and saw his shopping cart where he kept his belongings, but he was nowhere to be found. When I started up the car to drive off, I glanced in my rear view mirror and saw these eyes staring in the car through the rear window.

It made me jump when the man came around and said, "How can I help you?"

I said, "Damn Mr. Jones, you scared the crap out of me." I held my hand over my heart trying to keep it from jumping out. He looked at me for a split second and recognized me.

"Hey Joey, little miss Brooke's husband."

I said, "Yeah."

He said, "Sorry, I was just coming from a gas station where I get to use the restroom. I saw this car parked in front of my father's house, so I peeked in to see who was here and why." I looked at him a little confused.

"Father's house? You mean the church?" I asked.

He laughed and said, "Yes sir, why do you think I choose to sleep here? I feel safe when I'm near Him. He's protected me all these years on the streets so I can't complain."

All I could say was, "I guess that makes sense."

"So Joey, what brings you by?"

I said, "Well I just wanted to thank you for what you said about Brooke at the service. If anyone captured who Brooke was, it was you."

He said, "Son, you don't have to thank me. I meant every word, she was an angel."

I grabbed the coffee and said, "Well, I just wanted to bring you a cup of coffee... to say thanks."

He gave me a huge smile and looked up saying, "Thank you lord." I thought to myself, *I bought him the cup of coffee, why is he thanking God.* "I tried getting a free cup of warm coffee from the gas station. It's a little chilly this morning. The man working at the gas station, said the complimentary coffee was for customers only. I walked away saying, 'God, a warm cup of coffee would've been nice'. And here you are with a warm cup of coffee. God is great, wouldn't you say?"

"If you say so... well I got to go," I replied. He looked in the back seat and saw Sara.

"This is the little one…" As Sara stared at this elderly homeless man, he said, "She has her mother's beautiful green eyes." I looked at Sara, then at him.

"I know; I see Brooke every time I look into them."

"Miss Brooke believed in Jesus so much; I take it you don't?"

I didn't even look at him as I answered, "Billy I got to get to work. Hope you enjoy the coffee."

"Thanks Joey, have a blessed day."

I drove off thinking, *why is God always thrown in my face? Even for something as simple as a cup of coffee.* By the time I showed up at our shop, Carroll and Phil were already in the conference room talking. I put Sara, who was still strapped into her car seat carrier, on the conference table. Carroll unstrapped her and picked her up. "How is your daddy doing?" she asked Sara as she kissed her on the cheek. Sara was ecstatic to see Carroll. I thought it made sense because she was the one who's been taking care of Sara almost since the time she was born.

"Carroll we have to figure out a babysitting situation; I've got a lot to do here. I was gone so long, tied up with Brooke in the hospital." I looked at Phil and asked, "How are we doing with our projects and when do we meet these investors for the new projects?"

"Whoa there Joe, everything is fine. All the projects we are currently on are on schedule and we just wrapped up a big one in Port Orchard. I'll call the investors and set something up for Friday. Joe it's under control; you really don't have to be here. All I need you for is when we actually meet the investors. Go home, take care of Sara." I stormed out of the conference room, walking through the warehouse looking around.

"Phil these parts have been sitting here for two months, shouldn't they be on the jobsite?" I walked into the office, looked at the bid board, and started erasing the completed projects. "The bid board hasn't been updated, things are unorganized—I'm definitely needed back here. Carroll can you watch Sara while Phil and I stop by a few jobsites so I can see what our progress is?"

"Joey you can't just come in here and start barking out orders," Carroll snapped, "Who do you think you are?" Phil touched her on the shoulder, gesturing for her to let him say something.

"Joe, I know you're upset, but try not to take it out on us. You're going through some changes in life and its tough son, but you can't run away from your pain, or your daughter, and throw yourself into work. Joe please go home, spend some time with your daughter, and

I'll call and let you know when the meeting is with the investors."
I began to say something, but Phil walked over and put his hand on
my shoulder, "Come on Joe… for Brooke. She wouldn't want this."
He looked over at Carroll who had angry tears in her eyes. "What do
you say? Take some time. Believe it or not, after thirty years in this
business, I've learned a thing or two along the way." He smacked me
on the shoulder, making me smile as I looked at my sister with tears
in her eyes.

"I'm sorry Sis," I offered.

She looked at me sternly and said, "It's all right Joey, but next time
you boss me around I'll knock your head off." She held up a fist, and
Phil let out a loud laugh.

"I think she means it Joe," Phil teased.

"Oh, I know she does," I smiled and we all laughed.

As I walked out of the building to the car, I wondered what I was
going to do with Sara all day. After strapping her in, I came around,
jumped in the car, and looked in the rear view mirror at my daughter. I
pondered what Phil had said to me, that I can't run away from my pain
or Sara. *I don't want to run away from Sara, I love her,* I thought as I drove
off. *I just want to stay busy to keep my mind off not having Brooke around. I*

can't seem to adjust to her being gone. I looked in the rear view mirror and into Sara's eyes. Seeing Brooke in those dazzling green eyes caused my eyes to fill with tears.

"Daddy's here, I'll always be here my precious daughter, and I'm not running anywhere."

A couple of weeks had passed and I was spending every day with Sara. It was a huge undertaking, but I was hanging in there. I even got use to changing diapers without stuffing my nose with tissues. I was proud of myself. Brooke would've been proud of me too. Sure, there were times when I wanted to sleep through the night and couldn't, or when she got fussy it was tough to find the right way to rock her back to sleep. I found a great solution one night when she just wouldn't stop crying. I was just about to go nuts, but I noticed that every time we drove somewhere, she never cried or got fussy. So, that night, I packed her in her car seat and drove around town. Within ten minutes she quieted down. *Bingo,* I smiled as I watched her eyelids begin to flutter and drop as she fought sleep—sniffling a little from all the crying. I got her home and into her crib, still fast asleep. I got to know her facial expressions and her favorite foods—she loved smashed bananas with honey and hated smashed peaches. I learned that one the hard way when she spit it all back up all over me. I got to know what her favorite toy was. She played with most of the toys, but the one she always came back to was the stuffed monkey with long legs and arms that she could tangle herself into as she slept. The funny thing was, Brooke had picked that stuffed monkey out for her while she was pregnant, saying how cute and comfy it looked. I remember her holding it to her swollen belly, telling our unborn child, "You're going to love it." I guess Brooke was right, because Sara sure did love that monkey.

Three and a half weeks had gone by. I got in the habit of taking Sara in her stroller for a half mile walk down by the lake where Brooke and I would spend a lot of time together. Sara loved it. I would hold her over the water while she touched it. She would look back at me in amazement as her hand would break through the water and send ripples out all around her. We both would stare in silence as the sun danced across the ripples of water; it was almost as if she understood the beauty of it, just like her mother. Suddenly, we were startled by the sounds of

Motley Crue's *Home Sweet Home* as it came blasting out of my cell phone. I fumbled, trying to hold Sara and grab my phone from my pocket.

"Hello."

"How's it going Joe?" came Phil's voice from the other end of the line.

"Great, just here down by the lake with Sara."

"That's good really good. I hope this isn't coming at a bad time, but in all honesty, after meeting the investors and them okaying the builds in downtown, we are getting a bit overloaded. I was wondering, if you still want to get back to work, I sure could use your help in overseeing some of the work load."

"Of course Phil, no problem. Let me talk with Carroll about finding a babysitter who can help, and I'll be there in the morning."

"That sounds great Joe. Until tomorrow then, see ya." I put the phone back in my pocket and picked Sara up. I looked at her and said, "Daddy's got to get back to the world of work my little angel. This will be our last full day together." I strolled home from the lake walking slower than usual, soaking in the cool breeze and the sunshine as Sara looked around with her usual inquisitive look. As cars drove by or people passed us walking their dogs, she would get so excited. I thought maybe I should get a puppy for Sara. I just wanted to enjoy this last day with her before I went back to the hustle and bustle of day to day. I'm glad Phil held his ground on me taking this time with Sara. I now knew the difference between having a baby, saying I'm a father, and actually taking care of a baby—being there to be a father, feeding her, holding her, changing her, knowing her quirky faces. I love her so much, and now that I've spent these last three and a half weeks with her every moment of the day, I'm not sure how I feel about leaving her. I smiled to myself; it wasn't long ago that I was scared to death of being alone with her, and now I'm not sure if I want to be away for more than five minutes.

When we got home, I turned on the water in the bathtub, waiting for it to get warm for Sara's bath. When I was done bathing her, I put on some warm pajamas and made her a bottle. I took her outside to the porch where Brooke and I would watch the sunset together. It was perfect timing; the sun was just about to kiss the mountains as it said goodnight. I sat there holding Sara as she drank her bottle. She stopped drinking her milk for a second and goo-ed as if she were telling me, 'I love you' before she went back to her bottle. I laid two fingers on her chin and said, "Thank you Brooke. Thank you for leaving a part of you behind for me to cherish, love, and remember. I looked up as the sun disappeared, leaving colors of hazy yellowish-orange with scattered clouds across the sky. I remembered that during sunsets just like this one, Brooke would always say that it was created by God's paint brush. I smiled at the memory of my wife and said out loud, "God's paint brush."

CHAPTER 6

The Fall

CARROLL HAD FOUND A BABYSITTER that would come to the house and watch Sara. I gave her the third degree, asking her all sorts of questions. I even hinted that I might have baby cams all over the house. Carroll gave me a nudge in the rib. I smiled and said, "Just joking... maybe."

The young lady, Julie—who was twenty-two years old—smiled nervously, looked at Carroll, and said, "I'll take the job." She seemed to genuinely like babies and automatically fell in love with Sara. This gave me some comfort about leaving my daughter with a complete stranger. I would have preferred to have Carroll watch her, but she was running the office and trying to work things out with Richard; she had a life of her own, and I didn't want to weigh her down with my responsibilities.

My third day back at work was a hectic one. I ran through five builds, sat with building inspectors on issues that needed fixing. While the inspector was explaining how my guys had installed the second floor framing incorrectly, all I could think about was how much I missed Sara—so much so that I smiled in the middle of the inspectors ranting and raving. He saw my smile and blurted out, "Do you think this is funny, Mr. Connelly? Well it's not! This is serious business. I can have this build shut down until further notice."

"Whoa," I said, trying to diffuse the situation, "I was just thinking about my daughter. I'm sorry buddy; no worries, we will fix these problems lickety split." I cracked a smile at Phil. He rolled his eyes knowing that those were my father's words. Phil stepped in—seeing how annoyed the inspector was getting—and patted him on the back, explaining our game plan for correcting the issues prior to the next inspection.

I walked away from them smiling, thinking that I couldn't wait until the day was over so that I could get home to see Sara. I walked out of the building to get away from the dusty air. A cool breeze hit me as soon as I stepped outside. I soaked it in with my eyes closed. I opened them, looking straight up, and there it was… the Space Needle. It was about seven or eight blocks away from the jobsite. Since I'd been coming to the city for certain builds, I've been averting my eyes to avoid looking at it. But, here it was on a clear day, staring right back at me. A pang of pain hit my stomach as I stood remembering how much Brooke loved it up there. I stared at it for the first time since Brooke passed away. It represented the first day we met, the day I proposed, and most of our anniversaries. All of the sudden, I wanted to hold Brooke, to somehow be near her. I looked back at Phil in the building still talking to the inspector. He saw the look on my face and gestured to the inspector to give him a moment.

"What's up Joe?" he asked as he walked outside.

"Phil, I need to go for a walk. I'll be back in an hour or two."

"Joe we got two more builds to stop by, not to mention traffic." As he was saying this, I kept my eyes on the Space Needle. He saw where my focus was and he got quiet. When I looked at him, he understood. "I'll take care of it, just call me when you're ready. I'll swing back for you."

"Don't worry about it Phil. I'll take the ferry back."

"Are you sure Joe? I have no problem coming back for you."

"Nah, I'll be fine."

"Okay, call if you change your mind." I nodded at him as I headed down the street in the direction of the Space Needle as if it was a magnet drawing me in.

When I got there, I paid for my ticket and headed up in the elevator. The closer I got to the top, the more my heart ached as memories of Brooke flooded my mind. I felt like coming up here would somehow make me feel closer to Brooke. As I reached the top, I hesitated before finally stepping out. I walked to the edge, leaned on the rail, and thought, *Brooke would have loved it up here today.* It was so clear that you could see for miles. I noticed people taking pictures of each other. I felt like I was in their way so I walked over to the west side of the building where the wind was always blowing with a certain intensity. This was where Brooke would come to talk to God, or 'be in his presence', as she would say. I stood there with the wind hitting me. I closed my eyes and thought about my wife. There was a part of me that wanted to believe she was somewhere out there—Heaven sounded nice. I thought about little Jimmy and how convinced he was that Heaven was where he was going. Brooke told him stories of Jesus' sacrifice for us, so all who believed could be with him in Heaven. He seemed so happy, and all of his fear about dying no longer plagued his thoughts. In all the years I spent going to church and reading the Bible with Brooke, I'd never felt or seen anything that made me believe that any of it was a legitimate truth. This bothered Brooke. She always said that she worried about my faith, or lack thereof.

I stood there looking up at the sky. I closed my eyes and whispered, "God you listened to my wife up here... if you're real, and she's with you, tell her how much I miss her and how much I love her." As I whispered, I held two fingers up into wind as it blew, picturing my wife. I smiled as I dropped my hand, remembering how upset she got the first time we were up here—when I inferred that her talking to God seemed a bit crazy. And here I was, talking to God. *People must think I'm crazy.* I held onto the rail as a gust of wind almost knocked me off my feet. It was clear and a little chilly out, but as the gust of wind hit me, I felt a warm sensation run through me like a charge but not quite a shock—more of a comforting feeling. All the hair on my arms stood up. I looked around and watched people walk past. No one seemed to have felt what I just felt. I looked up again and whispered, "God..." I shook my head and let out a laugh. *I'm losing it,* I thought. I headed to the door that led to the elevators. I looked out one more time, kissed my two fingers, pointed out towards the scenery, and said, "I miss you Brooke."

I sat on the ferry looking out the window on the ride to Bremerton. Phil was on that side of town already. I told him I'd give him a call as soon as the ferry pulled in, so he could give me a ride to the shop where my car is parked. He mentioned that Carroll had left a message for me to call her as soon as possible. I thought, *Sis probably just wants to nag me about not getting the fifty percent payment from the build on 10ᵗʰ Street*. We were already seventy-five percent done. *I'll call her when I'm at home*. The sun was about to set and the waters of the Sound made the air crisp and chilly. I thought, *a cup of coffee sounds good right about now*. I reached in my pocket, pulled out a dollar, and headed to the coffee machine. This time, there was no one trying to figure out the buttons on the machine. I smiled remembering the old couple, Harry and Rose, as I slid the dollar in the coffee machine. I walked outside sipping on my coffee and watching the Bremerton lights get closer and closer. I couldn't wait to get home to see Sara, and hold her. I love the way she reacts when I walk through the door. She lets out a bunch of baby noises and reaches out her arms for me. I love her so much.

We reached the docks and everyone on the ferry started to file out. I reached for my cell phone to call Phil. *Damn, my phone is dead*. I looked around for a pay phone. I saw one across the street and started heading that way when I heard honking from behind me. I moved out of the way and the honking continued. I turned ready to say, 'What's the problem buddy?', when I recognized Phil's truck. I smiled and walked over. I noticed that Phil didn't return my smile. *He's probably upset that he couldn't get a hold of me.* As I opened the door, I said, "I know, I know, my phone is dead. I'm sorry you sat out here waiting." When I shut the truck door and reached for the seat belt, I really noticed the look on Phil's face. "What is it, Phil?"

"Joe, its Sara." I let go of the seat belt and it snapped back.

"What about Sara?" I could feel my heart pounding in my chest. "She's at home with the babysitter. What's going on Phil, tell me?"

"I'm not sure, I don't have all the details, but Carroll is at the hospital with the babysitter and Sara."

I just stared at Phil with a glazed look on my face. "Let's get to..."

I didn't even finish my sentence when Phil said, "We're headed there now." I sat rigid in the seat. I didn't bother with the seat belt, I just wanted to get to Sara as fast as possible. We didn't talk the entire ride over to the hospital. Phil knew I was worried out of my mind, so he just drove as fast as he could to the hospital.

When he pulled up, I was out of the truck even before it came to a full stop. My heart was racing as fast as I was running. I got to the front desk and just as I was going to ask for Sara, I heard my name being called. I turned around and saw the babysitter, Julie. In three large steps I was in front of her. Before she could say a word, I asked sternly, "Where's Sara?"

"On the second floor… this way," she answered and we walked quickly to the elevator. The doors were closing when I saw Phil walking into the lobby. He was looking right and left; when our eyes locked, he just nodded knowing that I was in a hurry to get to Sara. Julie began telling me what happened.

"Joe I'm so sorry; it happened so fast. I went to the fridge while she was on the couch… she rolled off and hit her head on the coffee table. She has a cut on her forehead." I clenched my hands into fists, listening to her ramble on. "So I called Carroll and she came right over." Before she could go on, the doors opened and I was out of the elevator.

"Where am I going?" I barked at her.

She looked at me blankly, then answered, "Oh, room 215." I turned quickly and followed the hallway, looking up at the room numbers above the doors. That's when I caught a glimpse of Carroll through the opened door. I walked in immediately asking how Sara was.

"Shhh, keep it down. Sara's sleeping," Carroll responded. I walked in and saw my daughter lying in a crib-like incubator. I walked over to her and could only stare. My heart ached when I saw the three tiny stitches on the right side of her forehead. I wanted to pick her up and hold her so badly. I could tell she had been crying a lot. While she slept, she would let out little whimpers as her chest rose and fell with each breath she took.

I turned to Carroll and whispered, "What's the deal? She's stitched up, let's take her home." Carroll gestured for me to step out of the room into the hall. When we were out of the room, I continued, "And what's with the heart monitor?"

"I'm sure it's just their procedure," Carroll replied. I gave her a look, waiting for the answer to my other question. "Well, when we brought her to the hospital, she was bleeding a lot and crying. It also didn't help that Julie was hysterically crying too. I tried calling you, but it kept going straight to voicemail, so I called Phil and told him to have you call me. I didn't want to tell him what was happening because I didn't want you to find out second hand. After two hours, I finally called Phil and told him to get you here."

"Carroll, I already know all that. Why are you still here?" She looked at me as her eyes began to tear up.

"I... I'm not sure, but the doctor told me he needed to speak to her parents. I told him that her mother recently passed away and that I'm her aunt, but he insisted that unless there was signed consent by the parent, he couldn't divulge any information concerning Sara. What I do know is that they did a CAT scan just to ensure that she didn't break anything from the fall. I asked him twice if she's okay and he just looked at me and said, 'Let me know when her father gets here'." A few tears slid down her cheek as she said this.

Carroll's words settled in on me. I leaned back against the wall and shut my eyes. I thought, *what is going on here?* It felt like déjà vu. When I heard footsteps coming down the hall, I opened my eyes and Carroll nudged me. "Joey, here's the doctor."

When I looked in the direction of the footsteps, I saw a thin man, short in stature, wearing glasses. He looked to be of Asian descent. He walked up and said, "Mr. Connelly?" Looking in the direction of my sister as she nodded, he put his hand out; I didn't move. He just stared at me. Finally, I snapped out of it and put my hand in his, "Mr. Connelly, I'm Dr. Jacob Stevenson. Would you mind coming to my office so we can talk about Sara?"

"Sure," I answered as I started to follow. "Can my sister come?" He looked at her and smiled.

"As long as you're fine with it," he replied. We followed him to a very small office, then he gestured for us to have a seat. He asked if we cared for water or a cup of coffee.

"Dr. Stevenson, why can't I take my daughter home? What's going on? What's wrong?" I was on the edge of my seat, anxiety practically pouring from me. He sat back in his chair, looking at me intently, and took a deep breath.

"Mr. Connelly, your daughter was brought in with a minor contusion and laceration to her upper right temporal lobe—which only needed three stiches. After the description the young lady gave of the fall Sara took, we wanted to be certain that there were no fractures or breaks, so considering her size, we accomplished a full body CT scan." He paused for a brief moment before continuing. "After reviewing the results, there were no breaks or fractures and there was no major bruising or bleeding on the inner temporal lobe, so the contusion and laceration are surface wounds and will heal just fine."

I smiled, "Great Doc, thank you. Well…"

Before I could finish, he cut me off to continue, "Mr. Connelly there was something else that showed up on the CT scan," he paused again. I felt Carroll's hand grab mine. "There is a mass just below her shoulder on the left side of her chest." Carroll let out a gasp and broke down crying.

I stood up, "I'm taking my daughter home. She's fine. Your machine is wrong, it's wrong!" The doctor put his head down and then looked straight at me.

"We did the CT scan twice to be one hundred percent sure, Mr. Connelly. Please sit down so we can discuss the course of action needed." He didn't really have to ask me to sit down, I felt my knees go weak. I couldn't stand even if I wanted to. I just slumped down into the chair. "We will start by removing the tumor and accomplish testing on it. I'm sure it'll be fine." As he went on, I zoned out, remembering hearing all the same things about Brooke. "Mr. Connelly do you understand?"

I snapped out of my daze, "What?"

"I would like to schedule surgery for first thing in the morning. That's why I would like to keep Sara admitted, so we can prep her for surgery and run her labs."

"Surgery..." was all I could manage to say as I rubbed the back of my neck. Carroll settled herself and began asking questions.

"Excuse me Dr. Stevenson, what's the size of the tumor?"

"Roughly the size of a quarter," he responded.

"How long will she be in surgery? What are the risks?"

"She seems like a healthy child... the risks are low. Due to the location of the tumor, it is not in a difficult area to work with. I would say forty-five minutes, tops, with no complications." Carroll nodded her head, clearly deep in thought.

"Dr. Stevenson, Sara was in my sister-in-law's womb when she was diagnosed with breast cancer. She passed away just six weeks ago. Is there any chance…" Carroll put her head down as tears streamed down her face. Dr. Stevenson understood what she was asking.

"No, I don't believe so. There have been studies for such situations and the percentages are one in five hundred thousand. It's extremely rare, but I honestly can't say more on the subject. I'm a surgeon, not an oncologist." The doctor stood up and said, "Let me get these orders in for tomorrow." He looked at Carroll and I. "Don't worry, I'm sure everything will be fine."

As we walked down the hall back to Sara's room, Carroll looked at me and asked, "You alright Joey?"

"Why Sis, why is this happening to Sara? She's just a baby."

"Just pray and have faith that she will be fine."

"Pray! Pray to who Carroll? Oh that's right, the God that killed my wife! Now my daughter is laying in a hospital just six weeks after her mother died in one," I snapped at Carroll. She stopped walking and turned to face me.

"Joey don't be like that. Brooke believed and after all these years you're still so cynical. Mom and Dad believed in God; I accepted Jesus in my life, and I owe it all to Brooke. She helped me, guided me through some of the toughest times in my life when Richard and I separated. And prayer is what kept me sane and gave me peace. Why don't you accept that? You can't control everything around you. You have to give in, open your heart, let Him in."

"I'll let Him in when He proves to me He exists."

"Joey having faith means you don't need proof. Well, I'll pray for you and Sara anyway." She walked towards Sara's room, leaving me alone with her words.

I slumped my shoulders and followed her. I hated being angry toward Carroll. I was just tired of being told to have faith in something that seemed to be intent on breaking me. As I stepped in the room, Phil and Julie where sitting there. Carroll asked them to step out in the hall way; I guess she was going to tell them the news. Sara was still sleeping. I walked over to her and put my hand on her chest. Her breathing was more relaxed. I thought, *at least she looks comfortable.* Carroll poked her head in and whispered my name. I turned as she waved her hand, gesturing for me to step out of the room. When I met her in the hallway, Carroll let me know that she was going to take Julie home, and then she would be back.

"No, don't worry about it. Besides, I'm pretty sure the hospital rules only allow one person to stay after visiting hours," I said.

"Are you sure?"

"Yeah, I'm sure Sis." Before I knew it, Julie wrapped her arms around me saying how sorry she was. She had started crying again, and I made a face at Carroll. *Like I need this right now, seriously?* I thought. Carroll only offered a sad glance with a half-smile. Finally, I grabbed Julie by her shoulders and slowly pulled her off of me. I looked her in her eyes and said, "Hey, it's not your fault, okay? Carroll will take you home now." I turned her around and handed her off to Carroll.

As Carroll and Julie walked away, Phil stood in the background quietly. As soon as they were out of site, he walked over and put his hand on my shoulder.

"How you doing kid?" he asked. I shrugged.

"Not good Phil, not good."

"Don't worry Joe, God will be watching over her tomorrow," he said, squeezing my shoulder. I didn't have the strength to rebut the comment.

"I hope so," was all I could say. "Why don't you get out of here Phil? You have a long day tomorrow, especially without me there to help."

"I got it covered, but I'll still pop up tomorrow for support. Love you kid," he said, leaving me with a hug reminiscent of my father's. As Phil headed toward the elevators, I turned and walked back in the room where my daughter laid sleeping peacefully. I stood over her, wishing we were home. I soon found myself on my knees beside the crib, praying:

God, or Jesus, I know you're one in the same—

That's what Brooke always said anyway. Well, I

Know all I've done is deny you… I might not be one

Of your most diligent followers, but please

Help my Sara, let this be nothing more

Than a simple operation. You owe me!

You took my wife, her mother, you can't have Sara!

I'm begging you, stop punishing the ones I love,

Punish me, please God please.

As my head fell lower, the tears stopped tracing down my cheek and began hitting the floor—causing a small puddle of tear drops to gather at my knees. I stared at the puddle, whispering, "I give… I give. I need your help, God." When I heard a knock on the door, I wiped the tears from my face and jumped up. "Yes?" I said as I sniffled, feeling a little embarrassed. A nurse entered the room.

"I just wanted to check in on the little one. My chart says Sara Connelly, correct?"

"Yeah… yes, my daughter."

She walked in further and said, "My name is Yolanda. I'll be your daughter's nurse for this evening." She stood next to me and gazed at Sara. "Aww, she's so beautiful. I see they have her scheduled for surgery tomorrow. They wanted labs done, but it can wait until morning. I'll get the blood drawn at five-thirty. They'll have the results ready in thirty minutes. This way, we won't have to disturb sleeping beauty here. How's that sound?"

I smiled and said, "I'm sure she would appreciate that. Thanks."

Yolanda caressed Sara's head, "Your daddy loves you little one." She then turned to me, "I'm sorry for interrupting your prayer." I stumbled over my words, embarrassed that I had been caught.

"Oh… I… I wasn't praying."

"Don't be embarrassed, it's in times like these when our Father in Heaven hears us most." She walked toward the door and before she left, she turned to face me again. "She's going to be fine, just fine, Mr.

Connelly." I stood there feeling drained and somewhat comforted by the nurse's words. As I sat in the chair watching Sara sleep, my eyes grew heavier and heavier. I finally fell into a deep and uncomfortable sleep myself.

I woke up startled by the sound of crying. I jumped up. Sara's eyes were wide open with tears streaming down her chubby little cheeks. When I stood over her, she got quiet and stared at me with those dazzling eyes. I smiled as she stretched her arms out towards me. I reached down and picked her up, laying her head against my chest as she melted into my arms. It was home for the both of us. I rocked her back and forth, whispering, "Daddy loves you my Sara, and I'm not going to let anything happen to you."

The nurse showed up promptly at five-thirty that morning. Sara took a liking to her right away, as she kept trying to grab her necklace. Nurse Yolanda smiled and said, "She's a feisty one! Come on little one, let's get this out of the way so we can get you prepped and ready." She touched Sara's little nose, making her giggle.

The labs were done and Sara was prepped and ready for surgery. Carroll showed up at six-thirty wanting to see Sara before she went in. "How's Sara?" She asked as soon as she arrived.

"She's doing fine." I was relieved to see that she was carrying a cup holder with two cups of coffee and a white bag.

She handed me the coffee and said, "I also grabbed a breakfast sandwich for you." But, I wasn't hungry; my stomach was actually turning with anxiousness. I wanted this over and done with. I gave Carroll a wry, but gracious smile.

"Thanks for the coffee Sis, but I'm not hungry." She looked at me like she was going to say something, thought about it, decided against saying it with a shrug of her shoulders, and put the bag down on the chair between us.

Dr. Stevenson walked over to Carroll and I, and we both stood up. "Good morning. Sara is prepped and ready for surgery. Would you like to see her before we start the procedure?" We both eagerly said 'yes' and followed Dr. Stevenson through double doors and into another room. There was Sara, smiling and giggling as one of the nurses was making baby noises at her and rubbing her belly. Carroll walked up first and smiled at Sara. Sara immediately got excited and put her arms out, but the doctor said we couldn't pick her up because she already had an IV in and a tiny gown on. I watched as Carroll held her hand to Sara's head as she prayed.

When she was done, I leaned over and kissed Sara on her forehead and told her, "I'll see you in a bit Princess." Dr. Stevenson walked us out and assured us that she was in good hands. I still had a lump in my throat as Carroll and I walked back to our seats in the waiting room.

After pacing back and forth for what seemed like forever, finally Dr. Stevenson appeared through the large double doors—still wearing his mask and scrubs. I met him half way, anxiously asking how Sara was. "She's fine," he replied. Carroll smiled and thanked the doctor. He then explained the measures that were going to be taken next. "Let me begin by saying that the surgery was a complete success. The tumor was removed with no complications. There are, however, some concerns with the lab results. Sara's white blood cell count was very low... well, at least below normal. We are sending the removed mass for biopsy."

"What for? I thought you just said the surgery was a success." I asked.

"Yes, Mr. Connelly, but its normal procedure for us to run a biopsy on any mass removed. We should have the results back by tomorrow.

We're going to need Sara to stay overnight so that we can monitor her. We don't like releasing children her age so soon after a procedure like this."

Twenty minutes later, we were called to the recovery room. Sara woke up crying. Carroll and I comforted her and she started to calm down. The nurse came in to let us know that her room was almost ready. She was going up to the third floor. When we got up there, we were assigned to room 316. Carroll was holding Sara and giving her a bottle, trying to keep her from grabbing at the IV she was connected to. Carroll looked up at me and smiled. I gave my best shot at a smile, but I couldn't hide my fears about Dr. Stevenson's words. 'White blood cell count' and 'biopsy'—I was all too familiar with those terms. It seemed like just yesterday I was in a hospital with Brooke. Now, I'm here with my daughter.

"Sis, I'm going to the restroom. You alright with Sara?"

"I'm fine go ahead," she assured. I walked down the hall looking for the restroom when I came upon a nurse.

"Excuse me ma'am, can you tell me where the restroom is?"

"Yes, it's on the other side of the nurse's station," she said this with a flirtatious smile, staring intently at me. She looked to be about twenty-six or twenty-seven. She was petite girl with bleached blonde hair. I wasn't in the mood to be courteous.

"Thanks," was all I said before I turned and started to head in the direction of the restrooms.

"Who are you visiting? Hopefully I'm their nurse," she said. I didn't respond to her statement. I just made the left turn at the nurse's station and went into the men's restroom. I didn't have to use the restroom, I just needed a second alone. I couldn't breathe; I felt trapped and my heart was beating so hard that I felt like it was going to jump out of my chest. All I kept thinking was, *not again, please not again.*

When I got back to the room, Richard was sitting across from Carroll and Sara. He stood up as I entered the room.

"Hey Joe, how's it going? Well… I mean, well… I hope everything turns out fine." After stumbling all over his words, he put his hand out for me to shake. He's been uncomfortable around me ever since he cheated on Carroll.

"Well, Rich, I'm hanging in there."

"Joey you should go home, shower, change…oh and also get diapers and a change of clothes for Sara. These hospital diapers are starting to give her a rash," Carroll said. I looked at her holding Sara; she seemed so comfortable. I hesitated responding to her directions. She stared at me for a second, "Seriously? I watched her for almost seven months, go on."

I smirked, "Alright Sis." I kissed Sara and headed out.

As I pulled up to the house and turned off the engine, I thought about how this house held so many good memories for me: my parents and Carroll, Brooke, now Sara and I—and here it sits... empty. I walked in feeling tired and drained. Carrol's advice actually worked out great—a warm shower sounded nice. By the time I showered, changed, and grabbed diapers and clothes for Sara, an hour and a half had passed. I called Carroll and asked how was Sara doing. She said that she was fine and sleeping. That put my mind at ease.

I put the bag I packed for Sara in the back seat, started the engine, and noticed that I was almost out of gas. I drove to the gas station I normally go to. It was only three or four blocks away from Brooke's church. When I was done putting gas in the car, I pulled out of the station on my way back to the hospital, and saw Mr. Jones walking down the street. I pulled up next to him and said, "Mr. Jones, where you headed? He looked at me twice before he recognized who I was.

"Hey Joey, how you doing son?"

"So, so. You need a ride somewhere?"

"Nah I'm alright. I'll walk back to my stoop at my Father's house." I knew he meant the church. I urged him to get in the car.

"Come on, get in Mr. Jones."

"I'll get in, but cut out that Mr. Jones crap, just call me Billy."

"Okay Billy." I thought about Brooke and how she always took the time to stop by and give him something to eat. So I offered, "Hey Billy, you hungry?"

"You don't have to Joey, I'm fine, just fine."

I smiled and said, "Well I'm hungry, so I'm pulling into this burger stand. If you want anything, just order." The girl came over the speaker asking to take my order. "I'll take the bacon cheese burger meal with the special sauce." She repeated the order and asked if that would be all.

Billy cleared his throat and said, "Well that sure sounds good Joey. Would you mind if I had the same?" I smiled and told the girl on the other end of the speaker, "Make that two orders."

We pulled up in front of the church; Billy turned and thanked me. I replied, "No worries Billy." When he was half way out of my car, he turned and said, "Why don't you have a seat on the stoop with me while we eat?" I really wasn't hungry, I just wanted to get him some food.

"I'm alright Billy, I really have to be somewhere."

"Come on now, just a few minutes." He looked at me, then turned, and waved for me to follow.

I said, "Alright just for a few. I really got to get going." He sat down and tapped the concrete next to him. I took a deep breath and sat. I had put the bag in front of me and took out the burger, when Billy cleared his throat purposefully. I looked up from unwrapping the burger. He held his hand out with his head bowed. I looked at him and said, "I'm really in a hurry Billy."

"There's always time to be thankful," he replied. I shrugged, put down the burger, and put my hand in his. Then, he began his prayer:

Father in Heaven, I just want to thank you

For this young man's generosity and for blessing us

Both with a meal on these steps to your house. That

Is grander than any king and queen's dinner table. Bless this

Food that we are about to eat and bless those who

Are like me with someone like this young man. Who's

Filled with kindness and giving. It is through your grace

That I will eat a hearty meal this day... Amen

I repeated his 'amen'. We simultaneously reached for our burgers. I took one bite and put it back in the bag. I really wasn't hungry. I took a drink of my soda, thinking about his prayer. I haven't prayed before a meal since Brooke was in the hospital. I turned and said, "Billy those were eloquent words." He was in the middle of his last bite when he covered his mouth.

"Thanks Joey," he mumbled through the burger.

"Billy, why do you thank God? I bought you the food."

He swallowed and said, "You have to remember Joey, God puts us in all places at just the right time. You running into me was no accident. Who do you think put it in your heart to buy me this gourmet meal?" he said with a huge smile as he gulped down some of his soda. "It was God Joey." He looked up and said, "My Father knew I haven't had a meal in two days; that's why I was at the gas station. Sometimes they have stale donuts left from the morning, by the free coffee for customers. And some of the employees let me have what's left. But, there was none today."

"Then why did you turn me down the first time?"

"Well, Joey, I don't like being pitied. One of my sins is pride," he laughed. "My father is still working on me concerning that sin."

I took another sip of soda as I looked at my watch—two and a half hours had passed since I left the hospital. I stood up and said, "Billy, I gotta go." He frowned as he looked at my bag with all the fries and almost a full burger.

"Joey you barely touched your food."

"I guess I really wasn't that hungry." He stood up and put his hand out. I put mine in his and shook it.

"Joey, you've blessed me today my friend, and I truly am sorry about the loss of your wife. She was an angel." I turned and walked to the car. "By the way, where's the little one?" My stomach turned at his question.

"She's with my sister, Carroll."

"Oh, well give the little angel a kiss from Uncle Billy." I didn't feel like telling him about Sara being in the hospital; she would be out by tomorrow anyways.

I walked into Sara's hospital room. Carroll was holding Sara, while Richard read a golf magazine. Carroll said, "Well that took you long enough."

"I needed gas." I put down the bag and walked over to Carroll and Sara. "How is she, Sis?"

"She cried a little bit. She's still in some pain from the surgery. The nurse came in and gave her some pain medication." Sara was half asleep in Carroll's arms when I caressed the short dirty blonde hair that fell across her forehead. I asked Richard, "Have you and Carroll had anything to eat?"

"No, I'm not sure what Carroll wants to do."

"I'm not really hungry," Carroll answered for herself. I looked at Richard and could tell he was ready to get a bite. I told Carroll they should go ahead and get out of here.

"I brought a change of clothes and diapers for Sara. I'm fine. I'll be taking Sara home tomorrow anyways." Carroll looked at me unsure, then looked at Sara. I repeated, "Go on, Carroll. You and Rich get out of here go have dinner somewhere. Sara and I will be home tomorrow morning." Carroll finally conceded and gave Sara a kiss on the forehead as she fell asleep.

Carroll gently laid her down in the crib, walked over to me, "Joey you call me if you need anything." She kissed me on the cheek, Richard shook my hand, and then they were gone. I reached into Sara's bag, pulled out her favorite monkey, and laid it next to her as she slept.

I woke up uncomfortable in the same chair I slept in the day before, rubbed my eyes, and looked at my watch: six-thirty am. I stood up, looking over at Sara; she was still sleeping, her little hand holding onto the stuffed monkey's tail. I whispered, "Don't worry Princess, I'll have you home today." I peeked my head out of the door and stopped one of the nurses. "Hi. I'm Joe, Joe Connelly, Sara Connelly's father. I was told we could check out today, can you tell me what time we can leave?"

"Let me check on her status," the nurse replied. She walked over to the nurse's station and started typing into the computer. I could tell she was reading what was on the screen. She then got on the phone and was talking to someone. I was trying to listen in, but all I could make out was 'Connelly'. She finally hung up and headed back over to me. "Mr. Connelly, I was told that Dr. Stevenson wanted to personally come see how Sara was doing. He will brief you on Sara's lab results at that time." She turned to walk away.

"Hold on, miss. They gave us Sara's lab results yesterday."

"Well, Mr. Connelly, you'll just have to wait until the doctor arrives for more information. I'm truly sorry I can't help you any further."

Sara woke up a little fussy. I changed her diaper, as gently as possible. I knew she was still in pain from the surgery. I gave her a bottle and laid her in her little bed with her monkey. She seemed content. I looked at my watch and it was nine-thirty. I thought, *what the heck is taking so long?* Finally, the nurse showed up about ten minutes later.

"Mr. Connelly, Dr. Stevenson will see you now. There was a nurse standing outside the room. The first nurse turned to the other nurse and said, "Betty, please stay with Mr. Connelly's daughter until I come back." She then turned and said, "This way Mr. Connelly." I followed her, expecting to walk down the hall to the small office where we first talked to Dr. Stevenson. Instead, we took the elevator to the fifth floor where I continued to follow the nurse. She led me to a large office with a decent view of the Sound. I saw Dr. Stevenson standing on the right side of a large desk, and there was a gray-haired man wearing a white doctor's jacket looking over some papers in a brown folder. The nurse said, "Here he is doctor."

"Thanks Jennifer," Dr. Stevenson replied as he then came over and shook my hand. "Have a seat Mr. Connelly." I didn't sit down.

"Dr. Stevenson, what's going on? You told me yesterday that I would be leaving with Sara today."

"Have a seat, Mr. Connelly… please."

I nodded and sat in the chair. I stared at the man behind the desk; he acknowledged me, but it was Dr. Stevenson who did the introductions.

"Mr. Connelly, this is Doctor Noah Considine—one of our leading practitioners here at the hospital specializing in oncology. I stiffened in the chair as I heard those words. Then, Dr. Considine spoke.

"Mr. Connelly, I've received Sara's results from the biopsy," he paused, then said, "I also am aware your wife has recently passed from a long bout with breast cancer."

"Yes... a little over six weeks ago, but what does that have to do with Sara?"

He and Dr. Stevenson looked at each other, then Dr. Considine continued, "Well there has been research for many years now concerning patients diagnosed with cancer during pregnancy; although rare, it has been proven that the disease can infiltrate the umbilical cord that carries stem cells designed to fend off most diseases through the pregnancy." He paused again and looked at me. Dr. Stevenson was also watching me. I couldn't speak. I knew where he was going with his speech; I just kept thinking, *no... no... no!* I didn't want him to say those words—every fiber of my being was on edge. Then he continued, "Mr. Connelly, reading the report on the biopsy conducted on the tumor removed from your daughter's upper torso came back malignant. Now, we can..."

I cut him off, "I'm taking Sara home." They both looked at me. "Thank you doctors, but we will be going home now."

"Mr. Connelly, I'm not sure you..." I stood up quickly and the room began to spin. I felt all the blood rush to my head as everything went black.

CHAPTER 7

The Blood Test

I WOKE UP IN A hospital bed with an IV in my arm. I had started to sit up when Dr. Stevenson immediately said, "Lay back Mr. Connelly. You passed out. Looking you over, I would say you're malnourished and—"

"Hold on Doc, what about Sara?" I said, hoping that what I heard before was just part of a terrible dream. He looked at me with concerned eyes.

"We will talk about her as soon as we give you this Vitamin B shot and get you hydrated," he replied. I watched as he tapped the syringe before sticking the needle into my left shoulder. It stung a little as I laid my head back into a plastic sound that was supposed to be a pillow.

"What happened?" I asked.

"Well, Mr. Connelly, a combination of things. As I stated before, you're malnourished, dehydrated, and taking into consideration the amount of stress you've been under—going through the loss of a loved one and now the news about your daughter—in layman's terms, you were overwhelmed and passed out." With those words, I sat up again.

"I've got to see Sara."

"Mr. Connelly please, you're not helping anyone, especially your daughter, if you don't calm down. We've phoned your sister, and I believe she is with Sara as we speak."

I laid my head back down, feeling a little dizzy. I closed my eyes, covering my forehead with my left forearm, and felt a throbbing pain from the shot in my left shoulder as I moved. Suddenly, I heard footsteps walk into the room.

"Jacob, how's he doing?" The footsteps said.

Dr. Stevenson replied, "He's fine, just a little shaken up." I opened my eyes and peered out from under my forearm to see who Dr. Stevenson was talking to.

"Mr. Connelly, you gave us a bit of a scare back there," said Dr. Considine. Seeing him standing there, I noticed that he was freakishly tall. This time I sat up, ignoring Dr. Stevenson as he asked again for me to lay down.

I said, "Tell me about my daughter, please. What are you going to do for Sara?"

An hour went by, and the saline bag that was connected to my IV was empty. I called for a nurse, "Get this damn IV out of my arm so I can get to Sara." The nurse seemed nervous by how agitated I was; I didn't care, I just wanted to see my daughter. Finally, I was free. I jumped up to my feet and headed toward the elevator. The nurse murmured something, but I was moving fast and had no intention of waiting to see Sara. When I got to Sara's room, she was awake and in Carroll's arms. She seemed fine and was smiling. It broke my heart; *she has no idea what she has inside of her*, I thought. I cringed remembering what Brooke went through. *But how... how can I let them put Sara through that?* I pushed the thoughts aside as I reached for Sara. She let out a giggle as she put out her arms toward me. I couldn't help but smile at her. Carroll's eyes were bloodshot and puffy, as if she had been doing a lot of crying.

I heard someone from behind me say, in a very monotone voice, "Hey Joe, um... um... I'm so sorry. If there's anything I can do, I mean anything..." It was Richard. He touched me on the shoulder before going to stand behind Carroll and putting both hands on her shoulders. She reached up with one hand to touch his.

"Thanks Rich… thanks," I responded, and we all just stood there in silence, staring at Sara.

The next week passed by almost in a blink of an eye. There were different doctors stopping in and talking amongst themselves; then they transferred Sara to the same hospital Brooke was in. My stomach turned as I thought again of Sara being put through the same suffering that Brooke went through. I would ask questions to the many doctors that popped in and out, but none of them would give me a straight answer. One did mention that this was a rare case.

"We are trying to find a way to fight, or mitigate, this… well, this situation with minimal impact to Sara." I just stared at him. He nervously looked at his clipboard. "Um… well, Mr. Connelly, everything is going to work out. Dr. Considine is one of the best," he said this without looking at me, then headed out the door. I slumped into the chair beside Sara's crib-like hospital bed and watched her as she slept. My eyes watered as I leaned my head against her bed, and whispered, "Brooke, our baby girl needs a miracle." The tears broke through my eyelashes and streamed down my cheeks.

Two days later, Dr. Stevenson came to see Sara. He did his normal routine of checking her with his stethoscope and taking her temperature, and then he looked at the small incision where they had removed the tumor. He smiled as Sara reached to pull the stethoscope from his ears, as she usually does. This time, though, Dr. Stevenson turned to me and said, "Well, we have come up with a procedure that doesn't require chemotherapy. Dr. Considine has been communicating with a renowned oncologist in Japan, a Mr. Takahashi. He has dealt with a similar situation in Tokyo, where the mother had cancer while pregnant and the cancerous stem cells were passed to the fetus. I'll let Dr. Considine give you the details and discuss with you what tests we need in order to prep for this delicate procedure."

Three hours had passed before a nurse came to Sara's room and said, "Mr. Connelly, Dr. Considine would like to see you in the staff's conference room on the eleventh floor." I looked at Sara. The nurse smiled, "Don't worry, I'll stay with her the entire time." I managed a slight smile and thanked her.

I stood in the elevator, staring at the numbered buttons on the panel. I dreaded hearing what was going to be done to my little girl. I didn't realize there was a woman standing behind me until she cleared her throat. I snapped out of the trance I was in and pressed the number eleven button, then stepped back as she pressed the tenth floor button.

The eleventh button lit up and the elevator doors opened. I nervously stepped out into the hall. I had been on this floor before; it was decorated more like a business than a hospital. There were no hospital rooms on this floor, just offices and conference rooms.

I walked slowly down the hall, looking into rooms and wondering which conference room I was supposed to go to, when a lady wearing a white doctors coat caught me peeking into her office. When I turned to continue down the hall she asked, "Sir, can I help you?"

I replied, "Yes, if you don't mind. I'm looking for Dr. Considine or Dr. Stevenson."

She looked at me for a moment, then said, "Mr. Connelly." I looked at her surprised and uttered a meager 'yes'. "Follow me," she said as she led me to the other side of the floor and into a large conference room with a long mahogany table that easily fit twenty to twenty-two chairs around it. I looked around the room and there were multiple people sitting at the table with white coats on. One portly man rested his hands, fingers crossed, on his stomach like it was a rest area. Another man, who looked to be in his late sixties, was tapping his pencil on the table smiling at me as he leaned back in his chair. The third man seemed too young to be in the company of the rest of the group; he looked about my age, or even younger. He sat there looking at me, then broke into a slight smile and gestured for me to sit down. I sat opposite him at the large table. To my surprise, the woman who led me here sat down beside me. Dr. Stevenson sat on the right side at the end of the table, near where Dr. Considine was standing. There was a white screen set up next Dr. Considine and in front of Dr. Stevenson was a laptop.

Dr. Considine went around the room introducing the other doctors. "Mr. Connelly, this is Dr. Jack Berish, our most experienced anesthesiologist." He gestured toward the portly man. "Dr. David Gray, an oncologist who specializes in bone marrow transplants." Dr. Gray was the pencil tapper. Then, he gestured toward the youngest looking of the men, "This is Dr. Mike Stroud, our top pediatrician. He works in the cancer ward for children." Then, he looked passed me and said, "The lovely young lady to your left is Dr. Isabella Rossi." I hadn't really paid attention to the woman who led me to the conference room; I turned to her as he introduced me.

She smiled and said, "Nice to meet you, Mr. Connelly." Her brunette hair was pulled back into a tight ponytail, and she wore little-to-no makeup. She had blue eyes and surprisingly light brown skin—this being the Pacific Northwest after all. She couldn't have been over thirty. Even though she tried to dull down her youth and looks, the lack of makeup and ponytail only made her look younger.

Dr. Considine continued, "Dr. Rossi will be working with me. She just finished her training at John Hopkins and is on her way to becoming one of our best in oncology."

She let out a light laugh and said, "Thanks Noah, for the self-esteem boost."

Dr. Considine then looked over to Dr. Stevenson and nodded his head. Dr. Stevenson pressed a button on the laptop, and a power point presentation popped up onto the white screen. He then began explaining what Dr. Takahashi had accomplished in a case similar to Sara's. With each slide of the power point, he would explain the procedure and how it was the best option and safest route.

I finally spoke up and said, "Dr. Considine, all of this is fine; I really appreciate you walking me through every step, but quite honestly, I just want to hear that you're going to save my daughter's life. I've been through all of this before, and I just... I just..." I felt weak and tired. I didn't know what else to say. I was still in disbelief that Brooke is gone, and now here I am fighting for my daughter's life to the same monster. All I could think was, *where is God in all this.* I still don't understand why Brooke had this unyielding faith in Him, even until her last breath. As these thoughts ran through my mind, I stared blankly at the table, still not knowing what to say. Everyone around the table just stared at me.

Finally, Dr. Considine broke the silence. "Sara is far too young for chemotherapy. That would normally be the avenue we would take. Due to her age and size, we feel it's best to start at the origin of the cancer, in the bone marrow. And normally, we start with family members to see if there is a possible match. We will need a blood test from you to see how close of a match you are. We have Sara's blood already, but we are going to have to take some bone marrow tissue. The biopsy procedure is scheduled for tomorrow. I hate to say this Mr. Connelly, but Sara's cancer is the fast spreading kind." I twitched as he said the words; it felt as if I was hit in the stomach. He continued, "We feel it's in her best interest to get her on the registry list for a bone marrow transplant just in case there are no compatible family members. If your blood type and other characteristics line up, then we would take a tissue sample from you to see if you're compatible for the transplant."

All of the doctors at the table saw how my face lit up. "Well let's go! Do the blood test and the tissue sample today—" before I could continue, Dr. Considine looked at me with concerned eyes. He put his hand up to cut me off.

"Mr. Connelly, it's not quite that simple. It's a one-in-ten-thousand chance that a parent is a match. Siblings have a far greater probability of matching than parents do, unfortunately. Yes, there have been cases where a parent was a match, but it's rare."

"I understand Doc, but there's still a chance; so let's get started!"

Dr. Considine sighed, "Isabella, please take Mr. Connelly to the third floor for his blood test and write up the orders; you know what tests are needed."

Dr. Rossi replied, "Yes, and I'll put urgent on the analytical process for a quick turnaround." I thanked her with my eyes; she nodded and said, "Follow me Mr. Connelly." We entered a room with several chairs with arm rests on either side of them. "Have a seat Mr. Connelly," Dr. Rossi said.

"Which one?" I asked. She waived her hand, gesturing across the empty row of chairs with a grin. I cracked a smile, finding it somewhat funny myself. I sat down and noticed Dr. Rossi putting on gloves as she told one of the nurses, "I will take the labs." The nurse scurried off, and Dr. Rossi walked over with four tubes with my name and Sara's printed on the label.

"Afraid of needles?" Dr. Rossi asked.

"When I was ten," I replied. She smiled as she taped my left arm looking for the right vain.

"So, Dr. Rossi, what are the chances that I'm a match?" She met my eyes as she stuck the needle in my arm.

"You can unclench your hand now." She had kind eyes. "Well, Mr. Connelly, I don't want to get your hopes up; Dr. Considine did say how rare it is that parents match their children," she said with concern.

"But, there's a chance that I am, right? How long will it take for them to do the bone marrow transplant when they find that I'm a match?" Dr. Rossi snapped in the fourth tube, then looked down at me with intense blue eyes.

"I really don't know what to say Mr. Connelly, and I don't want to say something that isn't true. I hope you understand. These cases are very rare, and Sara's age and size makes this case even more complicated. I will be praying—" she stopped abruptly, then said, "I wouldn't be lying if I said that I hope you are a match." She took out the needle and put the last tube in the plastic holder.

"What were you going to say?" I asked her. She looked at me confused. "You were about to say something, then changed the words."

She put the plastic container on a metal cart, then answered, "In truth, I was going to say that I'll be praying for you." She looked at me pensively. It was then that I noticed a very delicate looking silver cross hanging just below her neckline. She noticed that my eyes fell on the cross she wore. She tried to hide the necklace behind her collared blouse.

"Why do you hide it?"

"Mr. Connelly, it is inappropriate for staff to discuss religion, or our beliefs, with patients," she said uncomfortably.

I smiled, "Well, I'm not a patient." She seemed intensely uncomfortable. "My wi… ife…" I stumbled over the word as I said it, the pain still fresh in the pit of my stomach, "My wife was a devout Christian." Dr. Rossi looked at me earnestly.

"I'm truly sorry about the loss of your wife, and… and now…" She couldn't get the words out. She didn't look like a doctor at that moment; she looked like a girl who couldn't deal with an uncomfortable situation. "Don't lose faith Mr. Connelly. Jesus is with you and your daughter. He will see you through this dark time in your life; he always finds a way to let the light in to guide us—especially when it seems almost too dark to find the way." I laughed loudly. She looked at me puzzled.

"You don't believe… you said your wife was Christian?"

"Yes, she was. She prayed every day for Him to guide her and to let His will be done. I heard her say many times, 'if this is what you want, My Lord, then so be it.' But, she didn't mean it. She tried to be humble and hoped that He, meaning God, would change His mind. There was no miracle, no grand opening of the Heavens. One day, she coughed up blood and then... then, she died. So, no, I'm not sure my belief is as strong as yours. If God truly does exist, then He must hate me. He took my parents, he took my wife, and now he's trying to take my daughter. Tell me what God would do that, especially to a baby!"

She looked at me with wide blue eyes, "I'm... I'm so sorry Mr. Connelly. I should have never brought it up." She took off her plastic gloves, hands trembling. I felt like a complete ass. I calmed myself down, stood up, and touched her arm.

"Hey Doc, I'm sorry. I didn't mean to get so worked up. It's just that I'm... I'm well, I don't know what I'm doing... or feeling for that matter. I just can't wrap my head around it. My wife is gone, my daughter just came into this world with a full life ahead of her, and now she's fighting for it. Honestly, I have prayed. I'm not sure if God is real or not, but if He is, then why is He doing this? Why?"

She turned to face me, her eyes filled with tears—some had just spilled over her bottom eyelid and were rolling down her lightly tanned cheek. As blue as her eyes were, they looked like the ocean had just crashed against the sand.

"Whoa, hey… I'm really sorry. Please don't cry. I'm an ass, I really am," I said. She wiped her eyes and cracked a smile.

"I don't know why I got so emotional. I guess I just felt the pain in your voice, and you have every right to be an ass with everything that's happened… and is happening." She wiped her eyes. "Don't stop."

"Don't stop what?"

"Praying." She gave me a genuine smile. "Let's get your blood to the lab so we can get this ball rolling."

"Yes, ma'am."

I made it back to Sara's room and found Carroll giving her a bottle. Sara's eyelids drooped as she drank her milk. I whispered, "Hey Sis, how she doing?" Sara heard my voice and her eyes popped wide open, never once letting go of her bottle. She tried goo-ing at me, but it came out muffled through the bottle. I smiled at her, caressing her head. Richard sat behind Carroll watching the TV. He looked at me and said, "Sorry, I'll turn it off."

"Its fine," I told him. He put down the control and continued watching the Seattle news at five.

I walked over to the window and noticed rain drops hitting the window. I stared out at the drizzle as it grew more intense. I heard Richard put the TV volume up a little.

"*Mystery at the Cemetery,*" the news anchor announced. "*Hundreds upon thousands of caterpillars have migrated to the Seattle cemetery. The head care-taker for the three-acre cemetery has his ground keepers fumigating. In his statement, 'they are eating all the flowers on the graves'.*"

Carroll hit Richard on his leg as she pointed at Sara. Putting a finger to her lips, she shushed him. He lowered the TV and whispered, "Weird..." I smiled thinking about how bossy Carroll can be. I knew better than anyone since I grew up with her.

Two days had passed, and I hadn't heard anything about the lab results other than that they took more blood yesterday. I asked why they needed more blood—they already took four tubes. The only response I got was, "Dr. Considine put orders in to draw more blood Mr. Connelly. I'll let him know you have questions." That was yester-day, and I still hadn't heard anything from him or Dr. Stevenson.

Carroll showed up this morning asking if I had heard anything. Carroll could tell I was losing my patience. She said, "Joey, go home, take a shower, and get a change of clothes. I'll sit here with Sara until you get back." I rubbed the back of my head, thinking, *I don't want to miss the doctors.* Carroll saw my hesitation. "Joey just go. I'll call you if something comes up." I just nodded and Sara let out a deep sigh as I left the room.

I didn't make it half way down the road before I saw Dr. Rossi pulled over staring at a flat rear tire. I pulled up behind her, and she stared into the car—not recognizing who the driver was. When I stepped out, I could see the immediate recognition wash over her. She looked puzzled at first, then gave me a slight smile.

"Hey Doc, everything alright here?" I asked.

She gave me a grudging grin, "Not exactly." She gestured towards her flat tire. I asked if she had a spare. The trunk was already open, so I walked over and lifted the carpet concealing the spare.

I said, "There she is." Dr. Rossi smiled at the comment.

"Mr. Connelly, you don't have to change the tire. I... I already called my Triple A provider; they should be here at any moment."

"I'll have this done in five minutes, and by the way, just call me Joe." I wasn't sure why I said that. I've never asked anyone at the hospital to call me Joe, and I've practically lived there for the past year. I guess, being outside of the hospital, 'Mr. Connelly' just seemed a little too formal for a tire changing conversation.

It took me more than five minutes to change the flat tire; I was done in about ten. I wiped off my hands and threw the flat into her trunk. She gave me a smile and said, "Thanks Mr. Conne——" I held up my hand to cut her off.

"I just changed your tire; I believe the formalities are over, wouldn't you say?"

Dr. Rossi smiled and said, "Thanks Joe." In the middle of thanking me, the tow truck pulled up. She walked over and explained to the driver that she was fine and could drive to the nearest tire shop. The tow truck drove off. She walked over to thank me again; I saw the opportunity to ask about my blood test.

"Dr. Rossi, what's the deal with the blood test? And why did they need to draw blood again yesterday?" She immediately stiffened at the question.

She stared at me for a moment then said, "I believe Dr. Considine was just verifying that the first test results were accurate and to ensure all steps are taken to determine your compatibility to Sara." I stared at her for a moment; she was holding onto her left arm nervously and wouldn't look directly at me.

"Are you sure that's all that's going on here?" I asked.

"Really Mr..." she paused, then finally met my gaze, "Joe, it's unprofessional for me to talk about lab results. The lead physician usually talks with patients or guardians concerning testing or lab results. I'm really sorry." She turned, hopped in her car, and before closing the door, she said, "Sorry, but I really have to go. I'll be back at the hospital in an hour and will be sure to let Dr. Stevenson know that you are interested in speaking with him." The car door slammed and she was off. I stared as she drove off thinking, *that was weird.*

Three hours had passed by the time I got back to the hospital. When I got there, both Sara and Carroll were sleeping. I nudged Carroll to wake her. She sat up startled, then saw me, and stretched her arms out asking what time it was.

"Two-thirty. How's Sara?"

Carroll said, "She's doing fine. The nurse came in and drew more blood. I had to hold Sara; she didn't like it at all. It took me forever to stop her from crying." A pang of pain shot through my stomach; I clenched my fist and walked out of the room, not saying anything to Carroll. I heard her whisper, "Joey, where are you going?" I didn't reply. I stormed to the elevator. When I got to the eleventh floor, I headed toward Dr. Considine's office. Standing in the doorway, I found him along with Dr. Stevenson and Dr. Rossi.

As soon as I entered the office, Dr. Considine sat up straight. It looked like he was going to say something, but I didn't give him the chance.

"What kind of crap is going on here? You take blood from me twice, then you take more from Sara, what the hell is going on? Will somebody tell me why you're putting my daughter and I through this? I need answers, and I need them now!" Dr. Rossi approached me slowly.

"Joe, please calm down."

"I asked you earlier and you didn't want to tell me." She backed away surprised by my tone. Finally, Dr. Considine stood up and came around his desk. Leaning against it, he asked me to sit down. "I'm good where I'm at," I shot at him. He sighed. Dr. Stevenson and Dr. Rossi were on either side of him, and they both seemed extremely anxious. Dr. Considine wore a concerned look, but still kept his composure.

"Mr. Connelly, I'm going to need you to sit down so that I can explain why we've had multiple blood samples taken." I stared at him defiantly. He sighed again and gestured toward the leather chair insistently. I relaxed my hands, looked at the three of them, and sat down. "Well, Mr. Connelly, let me start with the process of the blood sample testing. It starts by testing your blood's tissue samples for antigens; these are the markers for cells that stimulate antibody production so that we can see if there's a match. Since we are testing a paternal parent as a possible donor, its normal for us to include DNA testing. We find that the child has fifty percent of the father's DNA and fifty percent of the mother's. Then, we check blood type. These tests start lining up the compatibility of the donor to the applicant before we conduct a biopsy."

I could only stare at him as he got quiet.

"Forgive me... I'm not sure I understand the point of you explaining all this to me Doc."

"Well..." he began as he rubbed the back of his neck. I turned my attention to Dr. Stevenson and Dr. Rossi; they were both staring at the floor.

"Doc, what the hell is going on here? Is there something wrong? Is Sara not going to make it? Tell me, tell me now!" I yelled. A nurse and another doctor showed up in the doorway of the office.

"We're fine," Dr. Considine said acknowledging their concern. They nodded and left. "Mr. Connelly, the reason for retaking your and Sara's blood sample is that... they didn't match."

"Well okay, I was half expecting that. You said it was rare."

"Paternally, Mr. Connelly," he clarified. I stared at him for a moment, not understanding what he was saying. Then, the realization hit me like a Mac truck. I stood up, anger flooding every inch of my body.

"What the hell are you talking about? Sara's my daughter! Call your goddamn lab; have them recheck the blood!" I exploded.

"Mr. Connelly, we re-tested the first blood samples three times. We thought we must have mixed up the samples or that the samples somehow got contaminated, so we drew more blood from you and Sara; the results came back exactly the same."

My legs felt weak under me. I slumped back into the chair I was sitting in. "It can't be... it can't be true." I didn't realize I was saying this out loud until Dr. Rossi came over and touched me on the shoulder.

"I'm sorry," she said in a barely audible whisper. I shrugged her hand off and stood up again. Without a word, I just walked out. I went back to Sara's room. When I appeared in the doorway, Carroll was holding Sara.

"There's Daddy. Do you want Daddy?" Carroll cooed to Sara. Sara reached out her arms to me. I could only stand, rooted, in the doorway staring at Sara. *It can't be true... my entire life with Brooke was a lie? How could she? How could she?* My thoughts raced. Carroll looked at me concerned and asked, "Joey, are you okay? You look as white as a ghost."

I started backing away from the door. Carroll stood up, still holding Sara. "Joey," she tried. I turned and ran towards the elevator—the sound of Carroll yelling my name at my back. Dr. Rossi was stepping out of the elevator as I stepped in; she looked at me as I passed her. She then looked down the hall to Carroll who was still yelling my name. Dr. Rossi turned to say something to me, but I had already pushed the button in the elevator. The doors shut, breaking our eye contact. I paced back and forth inside the elevator, waiting to reach the lobby. I couldn't hold it in any longer.

"Damn it, damn it!" I yelled and punched the elevator door with all my might. The metal contraption shook before the doors opened to the lobby. I may have broken my hand, but I didn't feel it. I didn't feel anything besides disbelief and anger.

Standing outside the hospital, I felt the rain drops immediately begin to soak my clothes as I walked blindly to my car.

"Mr. Connelly! Joe... Joe!" I looked around as I heard my name being called. Dr. Rossi was walking briskly through the parking lot after me. I opened the car door, got in, started the engine, and drove off. I looked in my rearview mirror to see Dr. Rossi just standing there in the rain, watching as I sped away.

CHAPTER 8

Billy's Story

I DROVE FAST AND HARD——so fast that I could feel the tires lose traction with the road. I didn't care, I just wanted the damn hospital as far behind me as possible. "Damn you! Damn you Brooke! How could you?" I screamed as loud as I could——not realizing that I was now driving in the opposite direction of the oncoming traffic. Hearing a big rig honk several times snapped me out of the anger trance I was in. I swerved back into my lane and the rear tires of my car completely lost their grip on the road. The car spun out of control as I pressed the brake pedal as hard as I possibly could. The windshield was a blur of rain as the car spun in circle after circle. When I finally came to a dead stop on the side of the road, I jumped out of the car. There was a four-foot railing that the car had stopped just three feet away from. I walked up to the railing and looked over. It was at least a hundred-foot drop to the bottom. I began laughing hysterically.

"Come on God! You can do better than this! You killed my wife—who, by the way, was a cheating—" I stopped myself from saying what I was about to say. I still couldn't bring myself to bad mouth Brooke, even if Sara wasn't my daughter. The rain seemed to come down even harder, as I yelled at the storm clouds above me. "I'm right here God! Is that where you wanted me?" I asked as I pointed to the bottom of the drop.

A truck pulled up behind my car. A man lowered his window and asked, "You alright buddy?"

I laughed, "I'm doing just fine… just fine."

He just looked at me for a second, then said, "Well, if you slid off this road, count yourself lucky. I live about two miles up from here and every year, in weather like this, two to four poor souls slide off this road to their death. Well anyway, you take care now."

I stood there watching his taillights as he drove off, then looked at the railing and noticed all of the black tire marks that disappeared over the railing. That's when I realized, I was lucky—or was I? I honestly wasn't sure at that moment—maybe I wanted it all to be over. Why not? Everything I held dear to my heart was a complete lie. Brooke was unfaithful; if anyone were to say different, I would have punched their lights out, but Sara's not mine… she's not mine. I got back in my car, looked at the rail one more time, and drove off. I had no idea where I was going, but somehow I ended up one mile from the cemetery—almost as if I was drawn there. I drove up the hill to where Brooke was buried, by two big oak trees that looked as if they've been there over two hundred years. The rain was really coming down hard as I parked near one of the oak trees. I could see people walking to their cars after visiting loved ones. *Well this visit is less than pleasant,* I thought bitterly. I got out of the car and walked to Brooke's grave.

I noticed that people at other graves were using brooms to clean the stones. I thought, *that's a little weird in rain.* When I got closer to Brooke's grave, I noticed that the flowers on her grave were filled with caterpillars. They were eating holes through the flowers and crawling on top of her grave stone. I swiped the caterpillars off of her grave and moved the flowers aside. I realized why the other mourners where using brooms. The caterpillars seemed to be everywhere.

I stood there in the rain staring at Brooke's grave stone. I read what was written over and over again:

Beloved wife of Joey and mother of their beautiful baby girl, Sara.

Rest now, my angel, for you are in Heaven with God

And your mother, Sara, who waits for you with open arms.

You will always be in our hearts, love you always.

I repeated the words "beloved wife', and dropped to my knees, cursing under my breath. Then, I yelled at Brooke's headstone as if I were yelling at her. "Brooke, how could you? I loved you with every fiber of my being! Sara's not even mine! You made a fool of me. Are you laughing now that you're gone? You thought you were going to get away with it. Well, I found out who you really are—a liar, a cheater... a cheater!" Losing my breath, feeling mentally beaten and exhausted, I leaned forward and laid my head against Brooke's headstone. As tears rolled down my cheeks, I laid both hands against the stone. I just kept asking, "Why? Why Brooke? How could you? How could you?" Then, I turned and leaned my back against it, staring up at the sky as the rain continued to pounce upon my face. I felt dead inside. I slowly got up, turned, and looked at Brooke's grave. "This is the last time I come here." I turned and walked back to my car.

I drove off feeling the need to get drunk. I wound up at a small, hole-in-the-wall bar. I'd never been to this bar before, even though I'd driven by many times. It was more of a rough neck bar—mostly bikers. I didn't care; it was the first bar I came across so I parked and walked right in, ignoring the stares I was getting from other bar patrons. I sat at the bar and asked for a bottle of Jack Daniels. The bartender gave me a baffled look in response to my request. "I think you mean a glass of Jack Daniels."

I stared at him sternly and said, "Nope, I meant a bottle."

He laughed a little, "The bottle is a hundred and fifty dollars buddy." I glared at him, not inclined to laugh or joke around.

"I didn't ask for the cost, just bring the damn bottle." I reached in my back pocket, pulled out two hundred dollars and slammed it on the bar. The bartender smirked.

"Sure thing buddy." And with that, I began my descent into drunkenness. I poured glass after glass, trying to drink this nightmare away. The realization that Sara was not my daughter shook me to my core. I didn't realize how late it was; when I looked at my watch, it said eight-thirty. My cell phone rang and rang. I didn't feel like talking to anyone. I felt like I was falling and there was no way to stop myself from hitting the bottom.

I finished what was left in the Jack Daniel's bottle, stood up a little shaky on my feet, and headed for the door. I walked out and was greeted by a row of motorcycles. One of them caught my eye. I walked over to this really cool bike with a chromed out engine, high-hanging handle bars, and black skulls painted on the gas tank with a fiery red background. I walked around the bike admiring it. Then, being as intoxicated as I was, I sat on the bike. I put both hands on the handle bars, looked over to a few people hanging out in front of the bar, and asked, "What do you think? Looks good with me on it right?" Immediately, one of them turned and walked into the bar yelling, "Eddie! Eddie, there's some dude on your bike man, get out here!"

I looked toward the entrance of the bar as a group of guys came out, all wearing black leather vests. The one in front was a burly man about six-foot-five with a beard. He had numerous tattoos on his arms. Normally, I would be scared to death of guys like this, but I felt nothing. As they approached me, I had the dumbest smile on my face.

The six-foot-five guy walked over to me, looking like he was ready to kill, and said, "What the hell do you think you're doing on my bike?"

"I'm thinking of buying this bike," I slurred. "What's your price? Name it, it's yours." I stared at him with a smile as I said it.

He looked furious; he actually growled as he said, "Buddy unless you have a million dollars cash on you right now, I suggest you get off my ride."

"How about this 'buddy'," I said, sarcastically. "At least let me take it for a spin around the block." Then, this huge guy yanked me off the bike by my jacket collar and slammed me against the wall in front of the bar.

A bunch of the guys with him shouted, "Knock him out Big Eddie!" He held me against the wall; my feet barley touching the ground. I shouted right along with his friends, "Yeah, Big Eddie, knock me out. Come on 'buddy'." Eddie looked at me a little baffled as he held me against the wall.

"What's wrong with you man? You got some kind of death wish?" I just laughed, then grabbed him by his vest and continued to egg him on.

"Come on, beat the crap out of me. Come on!" He just stared at me in disbelief. An older-looking biker walked over and tapped him on the shoulder.

"Let him go Big Ed, it's not worth it, brother." Big Eddie slowly let go of my jacket. The older biker—with long graying hair and a gray beard—told them all to head back into the bar and get out of this rain.

"Come on guys, you afraid of a good fight? Well I'm right here," I shouted. "Come on!" I yelled as I kicked the wall.

The older biker walked over to me and said, "Son, I have no idea who you are or what you're going through, but getting the crap kicked out of you isn't going to help." He stared at me intently. "I see you're in pain brother, but this isn't the answer." He turned his head shaking off some of the rain from his long gray hair and began to walk back into the bar. I stood there in the rain, staring at his back and just before he stepped into the bar.

I asked, "What is the answer?"

He turned and smiled at me, "I don't know about you, but when I come to a bump in the road of life that is beyond my ability to deal with…" he looked up toward the sky, pointing his finger upwards, "I talk to the man upstairs." With that, he walked out of the rain and back into the bar.

I headed to my car repeating those words, "The man upstairs…the man upstairs." *I just can't seem to escape Him. He's everywhere.* I couldn't even get the crap beat out of me by a bunch of bikers because they have a Christian as their leader. I drove to the nearest liquor store, bought another bottle of Jack Daniels—this time for $32.99. I said those words again, "The man upstairs." With a bottle of Jack in hand, I was going to have a word with the man upstairs. I drove straight to Brooke's church.

I stumbled out of the car and made my way up the steps. I opened the bottle of Jack and took a swig as I stared at the cross above the large double doors leading into the church. "So. this is it God? My lot in life. Well you must know that Sara isn't my daughter. Brooke lied to me about everything, even you. That's why I don't believe; this whole thing is just a sham," I screamed at the cross. "Brooke was a whore and you knew it. Is this what you're selling here? A bunch of damn lies!" I yelled as I threw the bottle of Jack Daniels at the church doors. The bottle broke on impact, splattering the door with brown liquid.

I heard a voice yell, "What the heck is going on out here, garsh danget." I turned to see who was coming from around the side of the church. "Who the heck is it, and what's going on?" There was a brief pause. "Joey, is that you?"

"You're damn right it's me, and I'm here letting God know the truth about Brooke," I replied, slurring my words a bit.

"What's that son?" Billy asked.

"That she was a whore," I answered. Billy walked over to me swiftly; I never noticed how big of a man he was until now. He loomed just one foot from me and stared directly into my eyes.

"Boy, have you lost your mind? If I wasn't in front of my father's house, I would whoop the white off your butt. What the heck are you talking about, and why would you disrespect your wife who's passed on like this, tell me boy." He shook my shoulders as he shouted his question at me.

I don't know if it was because I was drunk, or because I needed to say it to someone else, but I screamed, "Sara's not mine…she's not mine!" Then, I slumped down onto the steps of the church and sobbed. Billy stood there staring down at me for a second. Then, he sat next to me.

"How do you know?"

"The hospital did blood tests, and I'm not the paternal parent."

"Why are you two getting blood tests?" I remembered that Billy didn't know. I ran through the whole story about Brooke passing on the cancer cells to Sara, and how we were trying to find a bone marrow donor.

"I was tested to see if I was a compatible match for her and the results showed that I am not her biological father," I explained. We both sat there quietly as he digested the information. He looked at me as I sat there with my head in my hands. He got up and walked to the side of the church. I heard a shuffling of bags. Then, he reappeared with a bottle in a brown paper bag. He sat back down, opened the bottle, took a swig, and passed it to me. I hesitated for only a second, then took a drink. "I thought you were Christian," I teased.

He smiled and said, "I am, and I love my father with all my being. But, he knows I'm human and that I have weaknesses. Besides, it looks like you wasted a perfectly good bottle back there," he gestured towards the doors.

"Well, thanks for the drink." He sat, deep in thought, for a moment.

"Joey, I'm sorry about Sara, but I knew your wife; no matter how brief it was, she had a shining soul that could not deceive." He paused, "I'm sure there's an explanation for this."

I began laughing insanely at his comment, tears streaming down my face.

"Sure thing Billy. 'Oops I accidently slept with another man, here's a baby! Oh, and by the way, you're not the father.' What kind of explanation is there, huh? Billy tell me!"

"I'm not sure, but there are things that happen in life that only that person can tell you. I'm sorry she's gone and that you can't get your answer, but for whatever reason, you're still that little girl's father. She's fighting for her life and you're out getting liquored up trying to find an answer that you may never get. You're all that little girl has in this world. Whatever happened, or has been done, is in the past and none of it is that little girl's fault." I grabbed the bottle from Billy's hand and took another drink.

"How the hell do I get past it Billy? I don't think I can ever look at Sara again without wondering who the father is."

Billy cleared his throat and said, "Joey, don't make the mistakes I've made in my life; sometimes you can't take back the wrongs you've done." Billy grabbed the bottle back, stood up, and looked up at the sky. The rain had stopped and the clouds opened up to reveal the moon and stars. "Beautiful," he whispered, then took a drink. "I had a family once, many years ago." He took another drink before he continued. "I was a restaurant owner—had a partner, Ray Robinson. We were successful; we had three restaurants in New Orleans and were in the middle of opening two more in Mississippi. Times were good for me." He went silent for a few minutes, and I could see the pain in his eyes as he remembered his past. "I had a wife and two kids—my wife Patricia, or Patty, my daughter, Nancy, and little Billy Junior—everyone just called him Junior." Billy put his head down, and I saw tears stream down his cheeks. I just sat there quietly, waiting for him to go on. He wiped the tears from his eyes, cleared his throat, and continued.

"I was fifty-two years old back then, a strong man who was well-respected in New Orleans. I was considered one of the leaders in the black community. I was a stern business man with ambition. Ray and I were going to open a chain of restaurants across the country: Billy-Rays Louisiana Cuisine. I was an arrogant man Joey. I felt entitled; I bullied my way through people and business. I went to church most Sundays. Everyone knew me; I would make donations to the church, and I felt I could do most anything I wanted. You see Joey, I was an adulterer—a lustful man. People knew, but said nothing to Patty, due to my stature in the community. I took all that I had for granted. I didn't spend time with my wife or my kids. I was too busy trying to build my business and chasing women. I thought the nice house, expensive cars, and the private schools made me a good husband and father. But I wasn't there; I was never there.

Junior would ask me if I was going to be at his soccer game on Saturday, and I would say, 'No son, Daddy has to make that money so you can have all these nice things'. He would just shake his head and say 'I understand Daddy'. Damn, I was such an idiot... damn." Billy took another drink, looked at me, and said, "My Nancy was a dancer, a ballet dancer. She was thirteen years old and doing dance recitals—dozens of them, and I only made it to one... just one." His voice trembled as he said this. "Finally, my wife found out about me and the other women and threatened to divorce me and leave with the kids. I laughed at her and told her to leave without the kids. I threatened her with my money and lawyers, saying that she would never win in court. I played golf with most of the judges in the county. She didn't leave. In the months that came after, she seemed dead inside. I didn't notice or care to notice. I actually made an attempt to make things right; I told her I would stop cheating and spend more time at home. She seemed hopeful, but I was traveling back and forth between New Orleans and Mississippi trying to get the next two restaurants off and running. Ray and I hired a realtor—a woman. She and I... well, we became familiar with each other and one thing led to another; you know what I mean. One weekend, I stayed at the Hilton near the new restaurant we were building in Mississippi. I told Patty, I would be working all weekend.

She showed up with the kids to surprise me. I was changing in the restroom when there was a knock at the door. The woman I was with answered the door. Patty shoved the woman out of the way. When I heard her voice, I stepped out of the restroom trying to explain, but it was no use. I was caught red handed. I stared at my kids who were standing just outside of the hotel room. They just stared right back at me with tears in their eyes. Patty screamed how much she hated me, and how I would regret this. She took the kids, got in her car, and drove off.

That was the last time I ever laid eyes on them. When I got back home, I expected Patty to have packed and left with the kids. But, to my surprise, nothing was different. All of the kids' clothes were still hanging in their closets and Patty's personal items were still in our bedroom. But, no one was home. I called Patty's best friend, Shirley. She said she hadn't heard from Patty. I started making phone calls to all of our friends and family, but no one knew where they were. Last they heard, she and the kids were going to Mississippi to surprise me.

Then there was a knock on door. I'll never forget the chill that ran down my spine when I opened the door to find two state police officers standing there. They told me they had traced the license plate of the car to this address. They said that it had been involved in a head on collision in Mississippi. They told me the bodies in the car were burned beyond recognition. They asked me to confirm their identities. They told me there was an adult female, a teenage female, and a young boy—they figured between seven and ten years old. I broke down completely, telling them, 'That was my wife's car. She was with my daughter who is thirteen years old, and my son Billy who is nine'. Then, they told me that they weren't quite sure it was an accident. I asked them, 'what the hell do you mean?' They said, the car swerved into an oncoming semi-truck at the last second. The truck driver didn't have time to brake or swerve to the right to get out of the way."

Billy stood in front of me a broken man, as he stared at me through teary eyes. "She killed herself and took my babies with her. That's my cross to bear. I drove my family away taking for granted my wife, my children, my blessings—to the point where I pushed her over the edge. I buried them, what was left of their bodies," as he said this, his fist clenched. "Then I left; I left it all behind. I walked away from my business, my home, the money, anything that reminded me of the sins that killed my family, the sins that my children paid for. I pray every day for God to forgive my wife Patty. I take full responsibility for what happened to them." He stood there with the pain still evident on his face, as if it had just happened yesterday. He took another drink, "That was fifteen years ago. I haven't told that story to another living soul."

I sat their speechless; I never would have guessed that Billy had a family. He sat back down next to me and passed me the bottle. I grabbed it and took a drink. I didn't know what to say. Then, Billy asked, "Do you understand? There's some mistakes in life that you can't take back or change. That little girl is lying there in the hospital, waiting for her daddy to be there. Now, that blood test don't mean nothing. Blood doesn't make a father. Holding that child when she needs you, being there in every part of her life, that is being a father. God chose you to be that little girl's father for whatever the reason. Now, I can't explain why any of this is happening to you, but you're at a crossroad in life, and you must choose the right path. I came to mine, and I paid the price. Don't do something you will regret for the rest of your life. Ask yourself, do you love Sara?" I stared at Billy. He repeated, "Do you love her?"

I dropped my head and whispered, "Yes... since the day she was born."

"Well, what the heck are you doing getting drunk with this old man? Go be with Sara, go be with *your* daughter." I stood up and so did Billy. I looked at him and said, "Thanks Billy." He put his hand on my shoulder and said, "I know you're not a big believer, but at least you're arguing with him; it's a start." I was headed toward my car when Billy added, "Joey, remember, when we find ourselves in a hole with no way out, that is when Jesus throws a rope in and pulls us out. This might not make sense now, I know, but God will give you the answers you're looking for." I just nodded my head—not really believing his last words. I got in my car and drove in the direction of the hospital.

CHAPTER 9

Saved by a Rose

I DROVE UP TO THE hospital dreading going inside. I didn't want to have to explain where I was or why I left. When I walked out of the elevator toward Sara's room, the first person I ran into was Phil. He greeted me with a hug and said, "Joe, what the heck is going on? Your sister's been going nuts since you left. What's up Joe?"

I just sighed and said, "Not much Phil. What are you doing here so late?"

He looked at his watch and said, "Late? Its only nine-fifteen," Carroll called me frantically saying you left and weren't answering your phone. I tried calling you too."

"I'm sorry Phil, I didn't mean to scare you guys; I just needed some alone time." I was further surprised when I walked into Sara's room and found Dr. Rossi there. Our eyes met briefly, before Carroll approached me immediately, with a scour look on her face and quietly asked me where I've been. I looked passed her to see Sara fast asleep.

Then, Carroll grabbed my arm and began tugging me out of the room. She pulled me out into the hallway by the elevators, far enough away from Sara's room that she wouldn't wake her. Then, she began her tirade of scolding and questioning me. "Joey what's gotten into you? Why did you leave like that?" I felt a pang of pain in the pit of my stomach seeing her eyes fill with tears. *My poor Sis; she's put up with a lot.*

"I'm sorry, I just have a lot on my mind; I didn't want to tell her what I had just found out. I gave Carroll a hug and apologized again. She stepped back and gave me an accusing look.

"My God, you smell like a brewery. Is this your way of dealing with this?" Before she could continue, we noticed Dr. Rossi walking toward us. Carroll wiped the tears from her eyes.

"I'm sorry to interrupt; I just wanted to let you know that I'll be leaving." She was talking to Carroll, not once letting her eyes find me. I stood quietly—still upset at her for not telling me the truth outside of the hospital when she had the flat tire.

She gave Carroll a hug, then turned to me, "You alright Joe?" she asked, looking at me inquisitively.

I shrugged. "As good as can be, I guess." I was really trying to hide how drunk I was. She gave me a sad look and said, "Well, Sara's still sleeping. I told the nurse to check on her in an hour or so." I just nodded; Carroll thanked her for staying with Sara and being so helpful. Dr. Rossi smiled at her, "Don't worry about it. It's my job to look after my patients, plus Sara's special to me."

When Dr. Rossi disappeared into the elevator, Carroll continued her questioning. "Joey, what's going on with you? Please tell me." I looked into her concerned eyes, but I just couldn't tell her. I was still digesting this information myself. I felt humiliated and embarrassed. I could have never guessed that Brooke was capable of this, but it was true; the results kept coming back the same. I started to get a headache and suddenly felt tired.

"Sis, can we get into this tomorrow? I'm tired, and I just want to get some sleep. Is that cool?" She was angry at first, then her face relaxed.

"Okay, but I'm your family, and what you did today was not normal. You can't break Joey. Sara needs you, I need you; this is killing me to. We have to stay strong and positive for Sara." I nodded in agreement.

"Okay Sis."

Carroll and Richard left. Phil was on his way out to, when he stopped me. "You alright kid?" Inside, I was screaming, *NO!!! My entire life with Brooke was a lie, a damn lie!*

Instead, I replied, "I'm fine, just drained from all of this." I waved my hand, gesturing the hospital in its entirety. When everyone was gone, I stood at the door to Sara's room for a minute or two before I walked in. I stood over Sara's bed, watching her sleep; she looked so peaceful. She didn't have a clue that she was fighting for her life. I couldn't help but think, *I must have really pissed someone off in another life; otherwise, why would this be happening to me. First, my wife dies of cancer; now, my daughter has cancer, and come to find out, she's not even my daughter. She's another man's baby.* I stood there staring at Sara's features, wondering who her real father was. My heart sank at the thought. But, oh how I loved her—since the first day I held her in my arms. I sat back in the chair near Sara's bed and fell into a restless sleep.

I woke up to Sara crying. I rubbed my eyes so that I could focus on what was going on. There was a nurse taking her temperature and checking her blood pressure. I stood up, but too quickly. I sat back down; my head was pounding. I had a terrible hangover. Finally, I managed to ask, "How is she?"

"Fine," the nurse answered, "I believe Dr. Stevenson will be here soon to speak with you." I just thanked her as I held my head.

Before she left, I asked, "By any chance, do you have any aspirin here?"

She laughed and said, "Honey, you know you're in a hospital right?"

I smirked and said, "So, is that a 'yes'?"

She smiled, "I'll be right back with your aspirin."

I had just finished changing Sara's diaper, when I heard someone walk through the door. When I turned, I expected to see Dr. Stevenson, but instead it was Dr. Rossi. She looked extremely nervous standing there in the doorway. She started with a cautious, "Good Morning." I wrapped up the diaper, walked over to the waste bin and threw it in.

"What's so good about it?" I replied. She was holding her left arm; I noticed she did that whenever she was nervous. She was about to speak, when I said, "Well, what's the story? I heard Dr. Stevenson is coming to see me."

She squeezed her left arm anxiously before saying, "We've seen a decline in Sara's blood pressure. We're not sure why, but we're going to need to take more blood samples."

"Heck no, no more blood samples. You've put her through too much already." She walked over to me, this time more sternly as she released her left arm.

"Look here, Mr. Connelly, our best interest is for Sara, and we're trying to see what's going on with her. You're not going to prevent us from trying to save her are you?" Her eyes turned a fiery blue as she stood there daring me to say something.

All I could do was say, "What happened to Joe?" She looked at me for a second, confused by my answer.

"Well, I'm sorry, but you put all of us through hell yesterday—especially your poor sister. Carroll kept asking what we told you. You know I can't tell her; it's against hospital rules if you're not the guardian of the patient."

"I know. Hey, I'm sorry if I offended you in anyway yesterday. I… I… just didn't expect to hear what I heard; I mean, I'm still in disbelief."

She put her head down and said, "I understand that it wasn't easy for any of us to tell you, but Noah… Dr. Considine said the hospital was required to divulge that information to you as you are the sole guardian of Sara."

I picked Sara up and said, "Okay, where are we going to take these blood samples." I felt bad as we headed to the elevator. Poor Sara was going to get poked by a needle again; I hated hearing her cry in pain.

While we were in the elevator, Dr. Rossi looked over at me, smiled and said, 'Don't worry. You look like you're the one that's going to get the needle."

Sara's blood work was done. I took her back to the room, still trying to calm her down. I gave her a bottle; it seemed to comfort her. I held her and rocked her gently as her little breaths fluttered—still showing how upset she was. I still wondered how Brooke could do this, and why she didn't tell me before she died. I was still angry inside, but what could I do? I can't ask Brooke why, aside from yelling at her grave. I'm all Sara has; I know I can't blame her no matter how upset I am. It's not her fault.

Sara was sleeping more than normal, which worried me. I called a nurse and asked her to contact Dr. Rossi or Dr. Stevenson. The nurse nodded and got on the phone. I went back to the room, thinking, *I need a shower*, remembering what Carroll said about me smelling like a brewery. I called Carroll and asked if she could come watch Sara while I went home to get cleaned up. She said she would be here in an hour.

Ten minutes later, the nurse came in saying that Dr. Considine wanted to speak with me in his office. She asked, "Do you know where it is?" I told her I did. She said, "I'll sit with Sara while you go." I thanked her and headed to the elevator. I felt anxious about what he was going to tell me this time; I just had a bad feeling in the pit of my stomach.

When I walked in to his office, Dr. Considine was sitting at his desk, and Doctor Rossi was leaning on the left corner. Dr. Considine asked, "How are you, Mr. Connelly?"

"I'm not sure Doc, after what you told me yesterday, how do you think I am?" He nodded in understanding.

"Mr. Connelly, I had Sara's blood drawn again due to some of her symptoms. She sleeps more and more, showing fatigue, which is not common in children her age. Also, her blood pressure is below normal." I waited for him to continue, but he fell silent in thought for a few seconds. "Mr. Connelly, it seems like the cancer cells are in a lymphatic state."

"What are you saying Doc?"

Dr. Rossi came and sat in the chair next to me and said, "It means it's spreading." I stood quietly for a moment.

"She's going to die isn't she?" Saying those words made me feel physically sick.

He replied, "She's not quite at that stage yet. If we don't find a donor match soon, her chances of surviving this drop with each passing day." Dr. Considine got up walked around his desk, then put his hand on my shoulder and said, "I'm sorry you're going through all of this. It can't be easy, especially with what we told you yesterday. Just try to stay as strong as you possibly can, for Sara."

I left the doctor's office feeling nauseated. When I got off the elevator on Sara's floor, I ran to the restroom and vomited. I stared into the toilet looking at all the alcohol I drank yesterday. I flushed the light brown substance down. Although the liquid was gone, the odor of stale Jack Daniels permeated the air. I washed my hands and face, rinsing my mouth out at the same time, then stood there staring at my reflection in the mirror. *What am I going to do?* I wondered. I headed back to Sara's room with a feeling of dread in the pit of my stomach. I realized there was nothing I could do to stop this. *Why is it that everyone I love is taken from me? My parents, Brooke… Now, I'm helpless, dying inside, at the thought of losing Sara—who, because of Brooke, is another man's child. Not mine… not mine.*

When I got back to Sara's room, Carroll was already sitting there holding her. "Hey Sis."

"What's wrong?" She asked immediately. I looked at Sara, not wanting to breakdown in front of Carroll.

"Nothing, I just don't feel well." She looked at me, trying to read me; she reminded me of Mom when she did this. Mom would always give us this look, trying to decide if we were lying or telling the truth.

"What did the doctor say?" Luckily, Dr. Mike Stroud walked in to check on Sara at that moment. He showed up almost daily, mostly to make Sara giggle while he looked her over. Sara definitely was entertained by Dr. Stroud, who insisted that I just call him Mike—good guy all-in-all.

Dr. Rossi was right behind him through the door. She and Carroll hugged; she asked Carroll how she was feeling today. Carroll smiled and said, "Fine. Thank you for staying and helping yesterday." Then, she made a face at me, letting Dr. Rossi know that I was what had her stressed out. She just smiled at Carroll, then turned and looked at me, her smile fading. She knew that I had every right to act the way I did, considering what I had just found out. Dr. Rossi jumped in to hold Sara while Dr. Stroud waved to us, saying that he would stop by later to check on her again. Watching Dr. Rossi with Sara was somewhat daunting. She held Sara so gently and lovingly. A fear ran through me as I thought, *is all this affection towards Sara because they know she's not going to make it?*

This realization made me stand up and want to ask her if she knew something more. I needed to talk to her alone; I didn't want to scare Carroll. "Carroll would you mind watching Sara while I have a word with the doctor in the hall?" Carroll looked at me and Dr. Rossi suspiciously. "Yeah sure. Uh... is everything alright?"

"Yes, I have just a few questions for the Doc." Once I had her alone, I asked, "What's going on? Is there something you're not telling me?"

"No, I'm not sure I know what you're talking about." I stared at her intently, trying to see if there was something she was hiding.

"I see the way you are with Sara, the attention you're giving her, almost as if you know she's not going to make it."

"Look, I can't even imagine or try to understand all of the pain and heartbreak you're going through right now. Yes, I'm giving Sara all of the extra care I can give her. She's just a baby; I'm not just a doctor, I'm human and I have a heart." She put her hands to her chest as she said this. "I'm sorry Joe, I'm really sorry. Yes, I am worried that time is running out for Sara, and it might show sometimes when I'm near her. But, we have a fighting chance; we are looking for a match around the clock. We have Sara's labs sent out around the country as urgent. So to answer your question, yes I'm worried, and yes Sara's situation is critical, but we can't give up hope. Sara's in my prayers every night."

I laughed, "What good are prayers? They just go into thin air." I could tell that she was upset by my comment

"Well, I sincerely hope that you are wrong." She turned to walk away. I could see I clearly upset her. Then, she turned and asked, "Have you told Carroll?" I knew what she was asking me.

"No I haven't. I still don't want to believe it myself." My domineering, angry father attitude disappeared; she saw that I was broken.

She walked back towards me, "I'm so sorry Joe. I'm not sure why all of this is happening to you." She touched my arm, trying to comfort me. "Please have faith, just have faith that everything will work out in the end." I didn't want to hear it, but I also didn't have the strength to argue with her.

"I'm sorry, I have no right to talk to you that way."

"It's understandable," she smiled. "You've been through a lot. I also believe that it would help if you confided in your sister. She loves you and she can help with all the baggage you're carrying around on your shoulders; sometimes it just helps to talk."

When I got back to the room, Sara was sleeping and Carroll was leaning her head against her bed; it looked like she was praying. She looked up when I walked in, and asked what that was about.

"Nothing, just asked about the progress on finding a donor. Everyone we know already gave blood, now the urgency went out nationwide." I looked at Carroll wondering what her reaction would be if I told her that Brooke had cheated on me, and that I wasn't Sara's biological father. The thought made me feel ill; I couldn't tell anyone. I was too embarrassed and I didn't want to tarnish the memory of Brooke, even if she did deserve it. The truth was, I still loved her.

I got up and told Carroll I needed a shower. She looked at me, waved her hand in front of her nose, and agreed.

"Very funny," I laughed.

"Go ahead," she smiled. "Richard should be getting here in a bit."

"I won't be long."

I felt somewhat refreshed after the shower. I was hungry and went into the kitchen. Opening the refrigerator door, I looked for something to eat and found a bad stench instead. I hadn't had any time to shop let alone throw bad food out. I just shut the fridge door and figured, *I'll get something to eat on the way back to the hospital.* I grabbed the car keys. Before walking out the door, I stopped and stared at the photo collage Brooke put together of us. In every photo she looked so happy; I genuinely believed she loved me; and never, ever would I have believed that she would be capable of doing something like this. I walked out, not wanting to look at photos of her—the pain was too fresh.

Walking into Sara's room, I just felt different now. I loved Sara; I knew that and she was an innocent child. But, she was also a reminder of Brooke's betrayal. I hated this feeling, but it was there and I couldn't shake it. Carroll was talking to Dr. Rossi when I walked in. Rich was watching TV as he always did while he was here with Carroll. Carroll turned smiling with teary eyes and told me that they might have a potential donor. A feeling of relief came over me. I looked at Dr. Rossi and asked, "Is it true?"

She replied, "Yes, we might have a match! There's a young woman in Texas that might be a match. We're waiting on the lab samples to confirm."

I let out a breath of relief and smiled, "Thank God." Carroll and Dr. Rossi both stared at me in disbelief at the words that had just fallen out of my mouth. "What? It's just a phrase," I told them, realizing why they had such bewildered looks on their faces.

I noticed that Carroll and Dr. Rossi were bonding—what gave it away was Carroll calling her Bella. I asked Carroll, "Who's Bella?"

"Dr. Rossi told me I can call her by her name," she smiled.

"Bella, like the Twilight books, seriously?" I teased, Dr. Rossi. The only reason why I knew this was because Brooke got caught up reading those novels, and then dragged me to see all the movies. I let out a laugh. Dr. Rossi gave me a stern, yet playful, glare.

"Well, my name is Isabella. I'm Italian. I grew up with my parents calling me Bella, so I went to school telling my friends to just call me Bella. Plus, I had the name well before those movies or books came out." I just smiled.

There was a buzzing coming from Dr. Rossi's white jacket; she went into her pocket and looked at her blackberry. She smiled, "The results are coming in. Dr. Considine asked us to come to his office." Carroll looked at me and the doctor, asking if she could come. Dr. Rossi answered, "It's up to the legal guardian."

"Of course, come on Sis."

There was a mixture of feelings in the air, excitement and anxiety, as we walked down the hall to Dr. Considine's office. Dr. Considine stood up and offered us all a seat. He said the results should be coming in any minute and everything seemed to be looking good. We all sat with anticipation. Carroll was smiling; Dr. Rossi also sported a grin. I was happy, yet sad; still hurt over the fact that I wasn't Sara's biological father.

The phone rang, Dr. Considine smiled at us, then answered. He said, "Yes, this is he." Then, he listened intently to what he was being told. There were a few 'yes's and 'I see's. Then he said, "Have they retested the tissue samples and HLA antigens? Maybe there was a false reading... I see... Thank you." As he hung up the phone, I could tell by his facial expression that it wasn't good news. He turned his attention to us and said, "It is with regret that I have to tell you, we don't have a match for Sara's transplant. I'm truly sorry." Carroll began crying; Dr. Rossi hugged Carroll with tears streaming down her cheeks. I sat there motionless; I couldn't move or speak. I felt like there was no hope, no way to save Sara. Just like Brooke, I have to watch Sara die.

I stood up, looked at Carroll, and said, "We have to accept that Sara's not going to make it."

Carroll stared at me as if I was a stranger, "What are you saying Joey?" Even though I said the words, I didn't want to believe them myself. I was angry, and I just wanted all of this pain to go away.

"I'm saying, why should we keep getting our hopes up? She's going to die just like Brooke. No matter how hard you pray or beg your God, she's still going to die." I turned and walked out, "I need to get some air." I got in the elevator, pressed the lobby button and could see Carroll trying to catch up to me. The last thing I heard before the elevator doors closed was, "Joey wait." My stomach was turning with fear. I felt like I was going to explode. *I'm not strong enough to deal with this.* My eyes began to tear up; I wiped them away thinking, *I'm not going to break.* How much can one man take before he breaks? *I just need air,* I thought. When I got outside, a cold gust of wind hit me. I breathed in deep, taking it in and trying to control my breathing.

I heard Carroll's voice yelling as she ran out of the hospital behind me. "Joey, what are you gonna do, run out on Sara again, like you did yesterday? What's wrong with you? It's like I don't even know you anymore. How could you say that about Sara, how could you? What would Brooke think if she knew you said that."

I snapped back, "Who cares what Brooke thinks! She's dead Carroll, she's dead! Don't you get it? She doesn't think anything anymore." I was thrown by Carroll's abrupt movement as she charged at me, crying and swinging her hand at my face. She slapped me across my left cheek. I managed to get a hold of both her hands. She was crying and trying to get free.

"I can't believe you're my brother you bast——"

I cut her off by yelling, "Sara's not my daughter Carroll, she's not mine!" Carroll stopped trying to break free of my hold; she stared at me for a moment. Her reaction threw me; her only reply to my admission was, "Oh." I slowly let go of her hands.

"How did you find out?" I looked at her shocked. *She already knows?*

"Through the blood samples they took from me to see if I was a possible donor." She noticed how I was looking at her; she went from angry and trying to scratch my eyes out to being nervous. I stared at my sister intently, wondering why her demeanor had changed so drastically from one moment to the next. I asked, "You already knew didn't you? You knew and you didn't tell me!"

"Joey, I just... I..." She stammered. "Okay, yes, I knew, but I swore not to tell you until——"

I cut her off, "You knew Brooke cheated on me? I can't believe this Carroll! Why wouldn't you tell me, damn it, why?" I growled out this statement, furious with Carroll for keeping this betrayal from me.

"No, she didn't cheat on you Joey. You should know better; Brooke would never do such a thing."

I snapped back, "Then how the hell do you explain Sara not being my daughter?"

Carroll turned her back to me, as if what she had to say couldn't be said while looking directly at me. "Joey, Brooke was raped…" I was floored. *Why haven't I heard about this before? When? How? Why weren't the police involved?* All of these thoughts swirled in my head. Carroll turned to see my reaction.

"That doesn't make sense Carroll. Why wouldn't she tell me? Why were there no reports filed with the police? And why would she only tell you and ask you to lie to me, her husband? You're my sister, Carroll, why wouldn't you come to me as soon as you found out?" I felt just as betrayed by Carroll as I did by Brooke.

"Joey calm down, and I will explain."

I barked, "I'm calm! I'm calm, now explain!" Carroll looked at me, then looked off with a dazed expression as she replayed everything that happened the day Brooke told her.

"I was at work in the shop; you and Phil were on the new build in Tacoma." I nodded remembering the job in Tacoma. "I was knee deep working all the accounts we had and preparing invoices when the phone rang. It was Brooke; she sounded nervous and as if she had been crying. I asked her what was wrong, but she didn't want to tell me over the phone. She asked where you were. I asked if she wanted me to get ahold of you, but she said 'no'. Then, she asked if I could come to your house. I was a little freaked out by how she was acting, so I told her I was on my way.

When I got there, she was sitting on the porch crying. I ran to her, asking what was wrong and all she kept saying was, 'I couldn't do it, I couldn't do it'. I asked her, 'Do what?' She looked at me and said, 'Get an abortion'. I stepped back from her, not understanding why she would get an abortion if she was pregnant with your baby. She saw my reaction, and said, 'It's not what you think'. So, I stood quietly waiting for her to explain. That's when she told me she was raped. I grabbed her hand and said, 'Let's go tell Joey. Joey has to know'. But Brooke pulled away saying that it was her fault and no one would believe her. I was confused so I asked, 'what are you talking about, if you were raped, how is it your fault?

Then, she told me when it happened. It was three and a half weeks earlier. You had gone out of town for a builder's conference in Oregon and were gone for three days. She was working on reports at the college and..." Carroll stopped speaking for a moment.

"Why did you stop?"

"Well, she was asked to help one of her colleagues. He asked her if she would help him go pick up boxes of papers and files that were needed for one of the upcoming classes on campus. Brooke didn't think anything of it and said, 'not a problem'. She then told me that while they were in his apartment putting the files in boxes, he offered her a glass of wine, but she turned it down. The guy smiled and said, 'Water then?' she said, 'Sure water's fine.' She told me that she took a few drinks from the glass of water, and as she was putting files in the boxes, she began to feel light-headed, disorientated, and weak. She looked at her colleague and tried to ask what was in the water, but she heard herself speaking and noticed that her words were slurred. This colleague walked over to her and said 'nothing, it's just water'. Then he told her, 'My dear you don't look well, let me take you over to the couch.' She couldn't even walk; the man practically carried her to the couch. Brooke was crying the entire time she told me this Joey. I hate remembering how hard this was on her.

Then Brooke said he started undressing her and she was screaming inside. She hated his hands on her. He then walked over to his kitchen counter, poured a glass of wine, came back to her, and held her nose while forcing her to drink the wine. All the while he was saying, 'Can't forget the wine, my dear. This way we both know this was consensual'." My hands were clenched; my eyes were on fire. Carroll noticed my body language, but she still continued.

"Brooke couldn't breathe so she swallowed the wine. Not having any bodily control of herself, she said it was like having an out of body experience. Then, he had his way with her. When he was done, he dressed her and laid her down. She said he just sat there drinking a cup of coffee, waiting for her to regain her senses from the drug. When she did snap out of it, she began to scream at him that she was going to the police and would tell them that he raped her. He covered her mouth immediately saying, 'shh my darling. Really, I raped you here in my apartment that you willingly came to? Oh yeah, what about the wine on your breath that is coursing through your blood. By the way, where is your husband? Oh that's right, conveniently out of town.' He let go of her mouth. Brooke was dumbfounded. It was true. How would she explain all of this to the police and how would she explain it to you? Brooke sat there crying Joey; she was scared and didn't know what to do.

I then asked Brooke about proof of the physical rape. She said the drug had her weak and relaxed, plus he used lubricants. Brooke looked at me, Joey and said, 'Who would believe me, who?' I hugged her, feeling how trapped she was."

I was still angry that Brooke never told me and wondered how she knew that the baby wasn't mine. "Why would she get an abortion? Why did she automatically assume it wasn't mine?"

Carroll was cautious with her words. "I asked her why she thought the baby wasn't yours. I thought that maybe she just didn't want to take a chance on it being his. But, she told me you guys hadn't been using protection for a while and you both agreed that if she got pregnant it was meant to be. She said it was going on three years and she hadn't gotten pregnant. So, she went to see the doctor fearing she couldn't bear children. The doctor told her that she was very fertile and could have a baby whenever she wanted to.

That's when Brooke knew it was you, and she knew you knew how much she wanted a baby. So she didn't want to burden you with it. She just kept it to herself and thought maybe someday you guys would adopt. The day she found out she was pregnant, she cried and cried knowing it wasn't yours. She went to the abortion clinic signed in and sat there waiting for them to call her. And when they did, she didn't get up. They called her name three more times and she just sat there touching her belly, knowing she couldn't do it. It was a life and she couldn't take it. She got up and walked out of the clinic. That's when she called me." Carroll stared at me, waiting for my reaction to all of this new information. I had mixed emotions about it. I turned and leaned my head against my forearm on the wall in front of the hospital. Part of me was relieved that Brooke didn't cheat on me. But, why Brooke didn't confide in me hurt. Why wouldn't she confide in me?

Then, it hit me like a brick; Brooke's wake and Carroll's extreme disgust of Professor Rasmussen. How could she be disgusted with someone she had never met. Plus, Brooke knew the person. She was comfortable enough to go to his apartment like she'd done multiple times before. I'd even driven her there once. I turned and looked at Carroll with fire in my eyes, "Who did this Carroll? I know Brooke told you; who did this to her? I need to hear you say it." Carroll stared at the floor nervously. I grabbed her by her shoulders and asked again, "Who did this to Brooke?"

Carroll looked up at me with apologetic eyes, "I promised Joey."

"Damn your promise, now tell me!" Even though I knew who it was, deep in the pit of my stomach, I needed to hear his name.

Her voice trembled as she whispered, "It was the professor she worked for Joey, Professor Rasmussen." Carroll tried to tell me something else, but I was already running towards my car. I was furious. *I'm gonna kill him. I'm gonna kill him*, I thought as I sped out of the hospital parking lot. I could hear Carroll screaming for me to stop. It was too late; too much had been done and said. I was already speeding up the highway with only one person in mind.

I drove up to the house and ran directly to my room. I opened the closet door, reached to the top shelf, and pulled down a metal box. I stared at the box for a moment, noticing the rust and dust that was on it. I wiped the dust off and briskly walked to the kitchen, opening up the drawer that contained all the keys my dad had to every door and lock in the house. I tried every key to open the damn box. Finally, a key slid perfectly into the hole. I slowly turned it, opening the box and staring at my dad's gun. I remembered my dad showing it to me once, saying "This is only for protection son, for the family. Never use it if you don't have to…" Well I have to. I'm going to kill the man who raped my wife.

I got in my car, threw the gun on the passenger's seat, and headed toward the campus where he lived in the condos reserved for teachers and staff. I remember driving Brooke there and dropping off books he needed from the library. I clenched the steering wheel so hard my knuckles turned white. I drove hard and fast, pushing the engine to its limits. I drove up to the condos, grabbed the gun, and looked up at his window. The light was on; he was home. I got out of the car and walked towards the complex, shoving the gun into the back of my jeans and covering it with my shirt.

I got to his door and knocked; there was no answer. I knocked again. This time, I heard footsteps come towards the door. I stood off to the side of the eye hole in the door. I knocked again; he asked "Who is it?" It was him; I was sure of it. I knocked again. I could hear him slowly opening the door. When he peeked through the door, I saw that he had the chain at the top still hooked. He asked again, "Who is it?" I stepped in front of the door this time so that he could see me. "Oh, Mr. Connelly, I'm sorry, but you caught me at a bad time." He seemed extremely anxious. He tried closing the door abruptly, but I threw my shoulder into the door, breaking the chain and throwing him backward at the same time. I grabbed the gun from the back of my pants, and when he was getting his footing back, I hit him across the head with the butt of the gun, knocking him back to the floor.

I jumped on top of him and hit him three more times with the gun shouting, "You bastard, how could you do that to Brooke? I'm going to kill you!" I then pointed the gun at him. I had my finger on the trigger; he was moaning in pain. I didn't care as I watched the blood stream down his face. I shouted at him, "Look at me, look at me! You deserve this you bastard!" I continued to point the gun at him, yet I couldn't pull the trigger. He began begging me for his life, "No, no don't shoot." Hearing him beg angered me even more. "You didn't care enough to stop what you did to Brooke. Now you're begging me not to kill you?" I then cocked the trigger back. His eyes widened. All I kept telling myself was, *he has it coming, for what he did to my Brooke.*

"Joe… Joey, put the gun down Joey." I looked in the direction of the voice to find Phil standing at the door. *How the hell did he get here?*

"No Phil! I'm going to kill him! He raped Brooke. He ruined my life!"

"I know what he did, Joey. Carroll told me and she told me this is where I would find you. Now, put down the gun." I tensed up even more, putting the gun closer to his face. "No Joey, this isn't you." I looked at Phil with tears in my eyes.

"I have nothing left Phil. Why should I let him live? He took everything from me!"

"You have plenty Joey." He held out both of his arms, palms face down, as if to calm the situation. "You have Sara, who needs you, Carroll and me. Now, give me the gun Joe. I think he's done anyhow." Phil's gaze traveled passed me into the living room. I followed his eyes to a girl who was laying on the couch half naked, reaching her hand out toward us. I couldn't believe that I didn't notice her before; I was so focused on Rasmussen. I looked back at Phil who was now kneeling right beside me, holding his hand out. "Give it to me Joe, it's done." I slowly put the gun in Phil's hand. I physically crumbled once the weight of the gun left me. I shed tears of pain and relief, knowing that Brooke had never betrayed me. Phil put his arm around me and said, "It's alright kid, it's alright. You did the right thing." We both snapped out of it when we heard police sirens outside. Phil shoved the gun into his jacket and told me go see about the girl and cover her up. The professor tried to get up when I let him go. Phil stared him down, tapped the pocket where he put the gun and said, "You stay right there partner."

I walked over to the girl, who had her eyes open and could make slight movements, but was mostly incapacitated. I told her, "It's all right; you're going to be alright." The police walked in pointing their guns.

Professor Rasmussen started yelling, "He assaulted me, that man assaulted me." The officers looked at the situation, taking into account the girl who was half motionless on the couch and asked all of us to get on our knees. We did as they asked. One of the officers asked who each of us was and what was happening here.

I looked at Rasmussen and said, "He raped my wife, and I'm sure he was about to rape her." I gestured to the girl on the couch. The other officer was asking the girl on the couch questions; asking her to nod if the answer was 'yes'. When he asked her if what I was saying was true, she nodded. The officers looked at each other. Professor Rasmussen put his head down while the officer began handcuffing him.

The officers told Phil and I that we could stand, and asked us to follow them outside. They needed our statements; we agreed. When we walked out of the complex, there was an ambulance already there and what looked like a TV crew. When they brought the girl out covered in a gray blanket, the TV people ran to her asking questions. But, the police quickly began backing them away. The girl was coming around as they put her in the ambulance. She turned her head toward me and our eyes met; I could read her lips as she said, "Thank you." I responded with a slight nod.

The cops asked us how we got involved and how we knew the girl was there. "I didn't," I answered. I was here to confront him about raping my wife." I left the part out about wanting to kill him.

The cop laughed and said, "Well damn son, your timing couldn't have been better." Then he asked, "When can your wife come to the station so we can get a statement from her?"

"She passed away a couple of months ago from cancer." The cop put his head down, apologized, and looked toward the girl in the ambulance. "Well, I'm sure she would be proud of you for saving that girl." He then looked back at Phil and I, "Good job, I guess you guys can leave. We have your information. We will call if we need anything else."

Phil's truck was in the middle of the street. The police were looking inside and looking around for the owner. "Yeah that's me, I'm moving it now."

The officer nodded at Phil and asked me, "You okay to drive?" I looked at my hands; they were still trembling.

"Better not," I said. As I was getting into Phil's truck, one of the TV people came asking questions.

"Who are you, and what happened? Did you know the victim?"

I looked at the lady with the microphone and smiled, "No, ma'am. I don't know the victim. We're nobody, sorry." Phil smiled at my comment, tapped me on the shoulder and said, "Where to kid?"

"The hospital. I want to see Sara." While driving back to the hospital, I looked over at Phil and wondered how he had found me so quick. "So..." I said.

"Yes?" Phil replied.

"How did you find me so fast? I mean, I've only been here once with Brooke, and it wasn't easy to find even by memory."

He smiled, "That's the funny thing about it. Your sister called me, frantically telling me what happened. She told me that she researched this professor, after what Brooke told her, and decided that he shouldn't get away with it. She gave me the address that she got off the internet. The address she gave me was 2356 Longstreet Road. I was driving down Downey Avenue, headed to Longstreet Road. I ran into a road block; there was a huge tree that fell and was blocking the street. There were city workers turning cars around saying that we had to turn around and go down Longmire Road. So, I turned around and made a left on Longmire Road to find a way around to get to Longstreet Road. I was flying down the street, trying to get there before you did something you would regret." I just smirked at his remark. "When all of the sudden, this pooch comes running across the road in front of me. I swerved right and came to an abrupt stop almost hitting a parked car. When I looked up, I noticed that the parked car was yours. I'd know that Chevelle anywhere. I helped put the chassis on that car with your father. That's when I heard your voice and people started gathering outside of the apartment, for which the address is 2386. Honestly, I would have never found you in time if it weren't for that tree and dog." He smiled, "That's what I call Divine Intervention." I looked out the window and up toward the sky.

"Maybe you're right… maybe you're right."

When we arrived at the hospital, no one was in Sara's room. I walked over to the nurses' station and asked, "Where's my daughter, Sara?"

The nurse said, "Oh Mr. Connelly, I believe they're in surgery." I looked at her in disbelief.

"What? What do you mean surgery?"

She punched the tabs on the key board rapidly then confirmed, "Yes, she's in surgery on the second floor." I ran passed Phil to the elevator, telling him to come on. Once in the elevator, I pressed the number two button. The whole time I was asking myself, *what happened? Is Sara okay? Why haven't I heard from Carroll?* I reached in my pocket and grabbed my phone; it was busted. It must have happened when I slammed my body into Rasmussen's door. Phil looked at his phone and saw multiple missed calls from Carroll.

The elevator doors opened and I ran out, looking in every direction, trying to figure out the quickest way to get to Sara. Phil could see I was panicking; he walked over and asked about Sara Connelly.

The nurse said, "Oh yes, I'll walk you over to the waiting room. I believe the family is there now." The nurse walked us to the other side of the second floor; I wished she would walk faster. When she gestured that this was the waiting area, I walked passed her, looking around for a familiar face. I saw Carroll and our eyes locked immediately. Her eyes widened and then she ran towards me. She jumped into my arms hugging me.

"Joey, I'm so glad you're here." I hugged her tightly before I slowly pulled her away from me.

"Where's Sara? Why are they saying she's in surgery? Is she alright? What happened?"

"It all happened so fast. First, I was trying to find you. I called Uncle Phil to find you. I knew where you went, I just didn't want you to do something that well, you know what I mean. When I got back to the room, Richard told me that they had taken Sara to the prep room. I panicked. Richard told me that Dr. Rossi was with her, so I'm sure she's fine. Finally, Bella, well Dr. Rossi, came back to Sara's room——after I badgered the nurse for information several times. When she got here she told me what was going on," Carroll smiled. "They found a match Joey! I don't know how, but they did. Bella said it was someone local, and they had the person transferred from another hospital in Seattle." I exhaled a sigh of relief, and pulled her back in for a hug.

"Thank God, thank God. How long ago did they take Sara into surgery?"

"About thirty minutes ago, Dr. Rossi said she would update us when she could." I sat down in one of the hospital chairs, drained from all of the events that had just taken place. I felt sad, happy, grateful, and thankful all at once. These feelings were from all of the thoughts swirling around in my mind. Thoughts of what my poor wife went through living with this horrible secrete, then dealing with her cancer; I was happy at the thought that Brooke hadn't betrayed me and that the bastard who did this horrific crime against her was going to be punished. But, most of all Sara, my beautiful daughter Sara, was getting a second chance at life. I closed my eyes, leaned my head back, and for the first time, I was truly thankful. As I whispered the words 'thank you, thank you', I opened my eyes to find Carroll staring at me with teary eyes; she knew who I was thanking. I just smiled back, making no excuses this time. It was an unspoken truth that I had denied all my life, until this moment.

We sat in the waiting room for the next two or three hours, anxious for news on Sara. When Dr. Considine, Dr. Stevenson, and Dr. Rossi came through the door, we all stood up in unison. Dr. Considine's smile was a good sign as our tense bodies relaxed.

"Sara's in recovery. The bone marrow transplant went off without any real problems." Carroll let out a gasp as she cried. Dr. Rossi walked over to her and gave her a hug. "Please understand that we are not out of the woods yet. The stem cells have to start reproducing healthy blood cells, so she will be under observation for the next few weeks while we take more blood samples to ensure the HLA antigens are doing their job." Dr. Considine put out his hand towards me, but I was too happy for a hand shake. I gave the tall lanky doctor a hug. "Oh, well okay..." he said as he patted my back. Dr. Stevenson was next as I picked the short doctor up off the ground, thanking him. Richard and Phil shook the doctors' hands as they left the room.

Dr. Rossi approached me and said, "I'm happy we found a donor in time. You deserve some good news after what you've been through."

"Thanks for putting up with me. I know I wasn't exactly the easiest person to deal with."

"No you weren't." It looked like she was going to say something, but paused, then said, "Well, I'm going to check on Sara."

"When can I see her?"

"I will come get you when she wakes up."

"Sounds good." I put my hand out to shake hers. "Thanks for every-thing." She put her hand in mine and smiled. I was wondering why I felt so uncomfortable and wondered if I should give her a hug like I did the other doctors. "I really do appreciate all you've done for Sara," I con-tinued, her hand still in mine. She smiled. We both suddenly became aware that our hands were still connected. When we both released our hands, she smiled nervously.

"Well, I'll come get you when she's ready." I smiled, a little red in the face. As she turned to walk away, I asked who the donor was. "A sweet old lady who had a massive stroke today."

"Is she okay? Will I get the chance to thank her?"

"I'm sorry, but she had no brain activity. She was on life support when they brought her in. The hospital ran tests on her because she was identified as a donor. She gave every part of herself. They acted fast as soon as she came up as a perfect match for Sara. She died twice on the way here," she said sadly. "The medical team fought to keep her alive for the transplant. She passed away five minutes after we completed the surgery. She not only saved Sara, but her liver is going to a fourteen-year-old boy in San Francisco. Thank God the hospital was only ten miles away. If she was any further, they wouldn't have been able to get her here in time for the transplant."

I sat down thinking about everything that just happened—how Phil found me without having the right address, Sara's perfect donor. It almost seemed like a dream that I was afraid to wake up from. I looked around the room, taking in the people in it. Phil nodded his head and smiled at me; Richard was holding Carroll, comforting her, saying, "Sara's going to be fine." These were the people in my life, in Sara's life, and without them, I would have caved a long time ago. A feeling of love and appreciation washed over me. I was so thankful that they were in my life. I know Brooke was here with us; I could feel her. I whispered, "She's going to be alright Brooke, she's going to be alright."

Dr. Rossi came in to let us know that they had Sara settled now, and that we could come see her. "You just can't pick her up; she's still a little groggy." We all agreed that the terms were tough. As we headed to the elevators, I heard someone yelling at the nurse's station.

"I want to see my Rose. They took her, they took her!"

"Calm down Grandpa, we will find her." There was a young man talking with the nurse at the nurses' station along with the elderly man. Dr. Rossi walked over to the station to ask if everything was alright.

"They're asking for the donor they brought from the other hospital," the nurse explained.

The young man cut in, "Hi. Yes, my name is Michael. My grandmother had a stroke. We followed the ambulance to Harborview Medical Center. When we got there, they said she was on life support and that they would let us know when we could see her. An hour went by, but when I asked again, they said she was transferred to this hospital. Why would they bring my grandmother to a cancer hospital?"

"Her name was Rose Sullivan?" Dr. Rossi asked.

"Yes, that's my grandmother."

"Mikey, they took her. They took my Rose," the old man began again.

Dr. Rossi touched the young man on the shoulder. "I'm sorry, she passed away forty minutes ago."

"No, not my Rose, not my Rose," the old man pleaded. I started walking towards them. There was something familiar about the old man.

Carroll said in a low voice, "Joey, what are you doing?" I ignored her and kept moving closer to the nurse's station; I knew this man. As I got closer, I realized who he was; the old man from the ferry... the coffee machine. *That's right Harry... Harry that's his name. Rose, his wife... oh my God Rose. The sweet old lady from the ferry, she saved my Sara.* I stopped when I realized who he was. Poor Harry, he looked as if the world had ended—maybe it had. He had the same look that I had the day I lost Brooke. He looked so full of life when I met him, and oh how he loved his wife.

The young man hugged Harry as he wept. I could tell that Dr. Rossi was doing her best not to weep with him. She told the grandson that

Rose was a donor and that's why they brought her to this hospital. She turned to Harry, "She saved a little girl's life today, and a teenage boy in San Francisco. You should be very proud."

"I am proud. My Rose was always thinking of others. It just hurts to know that I won't hear her voice anymore or get to hold her hand as we take our evening stroll." Harry looked at Dr. Rossi, pleading, "Can I kiss her cheek? I haven't had a chance to be by her side since the ambulance took her, and for the last fifty-three years, not a day has gone by when I didn't kiss her on the cheek to say 'goodnight'." Dr. Rossi looked unsure about the request, but Harry pushed on, "Doc let an old man give the love of his life one last kiss on the cheek, for old time sake."

Dr. Rossi gave in, "Let's see what I can do, follow me." The grandson smiled at Harry with tears in his eyes as they followed Dr. Rossi down the hall for Rose's last kiss.

CHAPTER 10

The Letter

DR. ROSSI CAME BACK DOWN the hall with Harry's grandson. She apologized to us for keeping us waiting. "There's no need for that," I said. "I know what he's going through, it's hard letting go." She smiled at me.

Harry's grandson stood off to the side quietly. I walked over to him and said, "Sorry about your grandmother." He looked at me surprised; he must not have noticed we were standing by the elevators the entire time they were having the conversation about Rose.

"Thanks, my grandfather is really taking it hard. I don't think he's spent a day without her in the last fifty-three years." As he said this, I was gathering my thoughts on how to thank him and his family, especially Harry, for what Rose did for Sara. How do you thank someone for saving someone you love, when it was at the cost of their own loved one? Finally, the words came to me. I put my hand out.

"I'm Joe," I said introducing myself. He put his hand in mine.

"Michael." I began by telling him how I met his grandparents on the ferry to Bremerton from downtown Seattle. He looked at me surprised. "Really?"

"Yes, I actually helped your grandfather get your grandmother a cup of coffee—well, a cup of 'joe' as your grandfather called it." Michael smiled. "I take it you know why they brought your grandmother here."

"Yes, she donated bone marrow to a little girl named Sara; that's what the doctor told us."

"Yes," I paused for a moment then said, "Sara is my daughter." Michael stared at me with a look of astonishment in his eyes.

"Wow…"

"I know. So, when I realized that the woman who gave Sara a fighting chance, was the same woman I met on the ferry a couple of months ago, it really shocked me. I wanted to approach Harry and thank him for Rose, but it didn't seem like the right time. I just really wanted to say thanks for your grandmother's generosity as a donor."

"Thanks, she was the most loving, generous person you could ever meet, and I believe she wouldn't have had it any other way. She loved children." I smiled at him, shook his hand, and thanked him again. I gave him my number, asking him to call me in a few days, so that I could personally thank Harry for his wife saving Sara.

I had turned to walk away when he stopped me, "Hey Joe?"

I looked back. "Yeah."

"I just wanted to say, I believe this was my grandmother's purpose for being here. Here in Seattle I mean." I looked at him, puzzled by what he was saying. He saw my confusion. "My grandparents were not supposed to be here in Washington. They were supposed to go stay with my dad in Arizona. My grandparents were supposed to move in with my dad and mom after they were bought out of their home by city developers in New York. My dad had my old room ready for my grandparents to move in, but an electrical malfunction in the house caused a fire while my parents were out to dinner. When they got home, half the house was in flames. Thank God my dad had fire insurance. My parents have been living in a hotel paid for by the insurance company while they do repairs to the house. My parents should be moving back in next week, then they were going to send for my grandparents." I looked at him in disbelief. He just smiled and said, "The doctor told me that your daughter didn't have much time left to find a donor. I just believe it was fate that my grandmother was here to help your daughter." He patted me on my shoulder, "I better go check on my grandfather, God Bless Joe."

Dr. Rossi took us to the recovery room where we could see Sara. They only allowed Carroll and I in to see her. When we walked in, we could hear Sara crying; the sound of her crying tore threw me like a knife, and Carroll's expression told me she felt the same way. We both stood on either side of the crib-like medical bed. Dr. Rossi reminded us that we couldn't pick her up, which is very difficult when your child is in pain. Sara noticed Carroll and I looking at her and she immediately stopped crying. As I caressed her head, she let out short hiccupping breaths, the only remnant of her crying. She reached out her little chubby arms toward me to pick her up. Carroll's, "Aww, how cute," made me smile, but it took every fiber of my being to resist picking her up.

Sara was in the recovery room for another hour before they transferred her to an assigned room. Dr. Rossi said that Dr. Considine was going to have labs taken in the morning to ensure that the new stem cells were taking action by replacing the bad cells and reproducing new, healthy blood cells.

It was getting late, and I was physically and mentally exhausted. First, I asked Dr. Rossi to stay a moment; I had something to tell her.

I told Carroll, Richard, and Phil to head home. Carroll, as usual, gave me a problem—always making up an excuse to stay with Sara. I smiled at her, gave her a huge hug, and thanked her for everything she's done for Sara and I. I apologized for what I put her through the last two days. She nodded, understanding why I acted the way I did. I shook Richard's hand and thanked him also for being there for Carroll and supporting her through these tough times.

He nodded and said, "No worries Joe. That's what family is for." I smiled and patted him on the shoulder. I turned to Phil and shook his hand as he pulled me in for a hug.

I hugged him back, "Thank you, thank you for getting there on time."

He laughed, "Well, I had help finding you kid. You might want to be thanking someone else." He didn't say it, but I knew who he meant. I smiled at him.

"You're right, I have a lot to be thankful for, and maybe I should ask for some forgiveness also." Phil laughed out loud.

"That goes for all of us." Everyone laughed and said their goodbyes until the only ones left in Sara's room were Dr. Rossi and I. She stood over Sara's bed, watching her as she slept. I walked over and stood on the opposite side of the bed.

"You know this was a miracle?" Dr. Rossi said. "I mean, the way everything happened; I'm just… just well, in awe of it all."

"Normally, I would disagree with you, but even I can't deny that something special happened here today."

"Well, I hope you've found renewed faith, Joe. Hope, faith, love, God is all those things and more." I looked over Sara and remembered how much Brooke believed in Him—even up until her last breath. *How can I deny that something played a bigger part in all of today's events?* I can't explain it rationally—Phil finding me the way he did, saving the girl from that bastard, Rasmussen, and then Rose and Harry, who wouldn't even be here in Seattle if it weren't for an electrical fire. *Is all this coincidence or something more?* Those thoughts weighed heavy on me. "A penny for your thoughts?" she asked. I smiled at her.

"I'm just thinking, you're right; there's no other way to describe what's happened here. I can't rationally think of any other explanation."

"So, what did you want to tell me?"

"Oh yeah, um, well honestly, I just wanted to thank you for being there for my sister and Sara. I know I've been a royal pain in the ass for the last couple of days, and you never wavered in being there for us. I guess what I'm saying is, I'm sorry for any way that I've treated you, and I hope you can forgive me."

"There's nothing to forgive," she said smiling. I walked around Sara's bed to approach Dr. Rossi. I awkwardly put out my hand. She looked at my hand, smiled and said, "How about a hug? I could use one." She stepped into me, and I wrapped my arms around her. I could feel her body relax against mine; she was just as exhausted as I was. We let go and smiled at each other. "Well, I better go home and get some much needed sleep." I seconded her words with a yawn.

"Yes, sleep sounds good right about now." I stretched out my arms and finished a second yawn. I stared at Sara sleeping peacefully in her tiny bed. I whispered the words, "You're my daughter, and you always will be." As I said this, I only felt love and gratitude. I dropped to my knees at the side of her bed and thanked God openly, freely, and with a sincerity that I had been long lost until this very moment.

Morning came with sunshine and all its rays peeked through the blinds of the hospital room. The nurse had already drawn blood from Sara to run the post-op tests. Thank God they left the IV in, so Sara wasn't too inconvenienced by being poked by a needle. Carroll came with stuffed animals and treats for Sara.

"I'm not sure she can have any sweets yet, Sis," I told her.

"Nonsense, she's not diabetic. She can have a few."

Rich jumped in, "You see what I have to live with Joe." Carroll gave Rich a playful left hook to the stomach; he grimaced for a few seconds, then we all laughed. Rich gave Carroll a kiss on the cheek. "You still have a vicious left hook sexy lady." Carroll blushed and smiled. I made a sour face at them as I laughed.

We all turned our attention to the door when we heard a knock. It was Dr. Stevenson. "Good morning, Mr. Connelly and family. I have the results from Sara's blood test this morning." I stiffened a little.

"And... what are the results?" I asked. He paused for a brief moment, looking around the room before he said anything. "They're fine Dr. Stevenson. You can give me the results in front of them."

"You know the rules, Mr. Connelly, now that you've given consent—the results look good. The hematopoietic cells are already producing new marrow and blood cells. Of course, she will have to be monitored for several years ensuring that there's no relapse, but yes it looks like she will be in remission here pretty soon." The room lit up. I gave Dr. Stevenson another hug. He looked over Sara before he left. "Dr. Considine told me to say congratulations on the results; he couldn't be here. He's taken on another case of a ten-year-old boy with leukemia. He's meeting with the family now."

"No worries Doc, we understand." The mention of leukemia reminded me of Jimmy—I felt a touch of sadness in my chest. He was far too young to lose his life to cancer. I know he's in Heaven; there's no doubt in my mind. He was so full of life. Sara's cry snapped me out of my thoughts about Jimmy. Carroll sat Sara on her lap carefully, trying to calm her. Sara still had an IV in her arm that she continued to reach for. The nurses came up with a way to keep it out of her reach by putting it through the arm hole in her shirt and the IV tube came out the back of shirt behind her neck. Richard was holding the pink stuffed elephant in front of Sara trying to help Carroll calm her. Dr. Rossi walked in the room with a huge smile.

"I heard the good news!" she exclaimed.

"Yes, it is good news," I said returning her smile. Dr. Rossi noticed that Sara was fussy.

"Let me get her a bottle of juice, maybe that will help," she offered. When she came back with the bottle, Carroll passed Sara to Dr. Rossi. The bottle of apple juice did the trick; Sara was slowly relaxing. I caught Carroll and Rich looking at each other in a funny way, then Rich moved his head gesturing toward me.

"What's up with you two?" I said, letting them know that they'd been caught.

Carroll looked nervously at Dr. Rossi and asked, "Would you mind watching Sara while I have a talk with my brother?"

"Of course, take all the time you need," she answered.

"Why so serious Sis?" I asked.

"Let's go to the cafeteria for some coffee." I looked at Rich to see if he wanted to go. He looked at Carroll before answering.

"I'm good, go head Joe."

"Okay…" I gave Sara a kiss on her forehead while she drank her juice, then followed Carroll to the cafeteria. Once we had our cups of coffee, I watched Carroll as she added her sugar and creamer, wondering what she wanted to talk about. She picked a small table in the corner of the cafeteria. Once we sat down, I smiled. "So what's with all the covert operation tactics?"

"Well, it's not as much wanting to say something to you," she began, grimacing a little, "but more along the lines of giving you something." I shrugged my shoulders.

"Okay… give me what?" She reached in her purse, pulled out an envelope, and slowly put it on the table. I stared at the envelope, reading the words written on it. It simply said, *for Joey*. I recognized the handwriting; it was Brooke's. My smile faded as I asked Carroll how long she'd had this letter.

She looked at me nervously, "Brooke gave me this a few weeks before she died." I sat quietly, staring at the letter. Carroll finally broke the silence, "Joey, I'm sorry, but Brooke made me promise not to give you this letter unless—" she stopped mid-sentence.

"Unless what!?"

"Unless Sara got really sick the point of needing medical attention. Because then, you would need to know that Sara biologically wasn't yours so that she could receive the proper treatment, just in case there were blood tests involved. She told me that hopefully I would never have to give this letter to you. Brooke said she wanted to tell you so bad; she even tried, but she couldn't because you were dealing with so much already. She didn't want to burden you with more."

I stared at the letter that lay on the table, then moved my forefinger lightly over Brooke's writing, almost as if I was caressing her. Her writing was the last remnant of the hand that wrote these words; in some way, touching the words she wrote made me feel close to her. Carroll's eyes watered, "I'm sorry Joey, are you mad at me?" I looked at my sister, reached over to wipe a tear from her eye, and smiled.

"No Sis, I'm not. Thank you."

"Are you going to read it?" she asked, her relief was evident.

"Yes, but not here." I stood up and grabbed the letter. "I have to apologize to Brooke. I said some pretty bad things at her grave, and I need to make it right." Carroll nodded, understanding.

"Don't worry about Sara, I'll be with her."

When I arrived at the cemetery, there were signs all over saying: 'Do Not Disturb Cocoons'. Other signs said: 'Lepidopterology Study in Progress'. I had no idea what that meant. I parked and walked over to Brooke's grave; there were cocoons hanging from all of the headstones. They were everywhere. I stood in front of Brooke's grave, feeling ashamed of what I had said last time I was here. "Hi beautiful, well I guess I have a lot of apologizing to do. I'm so sorry, Brooke. How could I ever doubt you? I'm so sorry that I wasn't there to protect you from that monster. I'm so sorry baby. By the way, our baby girl is going to make it Brooke. You probably had a stern talk with God about it, knowing you." I smiled as I said this. "Carroll gave me this letter from you. I know it's about Sara, but she is mine and always will be. I just wanted you to hear it from me. And, the bastard who hurt you is finally paying for what he did to you, my love. I knelt down in front of Brooke's headstone, brushed away some of the cocoons that were on the ground, sat down and crossed my legs, then opened the letter.

My dearest Love,

If you're reading this letter, then you know that Sara isn't

yours. I don't know how much time has passed, but I know the

pain you're feeling is probably more than you can bear. I'm

so sorry I didn't tell you. I wanted to so bad. But, I was ter-

rified of what you would think of me. I know I am to blame

for putting myself in that situation. I'm so sorry Joey.

I looked away from the letter as my eyes filled with tears. "It wasn't your fault beautiful, it wasn't your fault. I'm so sorry you had to endure this pain alone. I wish you would have told me Brooke." I wiped the tears from my eyes and continued to read the letter:

So many times, I wanted to tell you what happened, so many times.

In the end, I knew I couldn't. I was dying, and I couldn't burden

you with more heartache than what you were going through already.

It's important for you to know that I have no regrets about walk-

ing out of the abortion clinic that day. The day the doctor put Sara

in my arms, I knew that I was meant to be her mother, and most

of all, that you were meant to be her father. You were so happy when Sara was born that I couldn't bring myself to ruin the joy you felt. Joey, it's not her fault, please don't look at her any differently than you did the day she was born. I believe she's a gift from God. He gave her to us Joey. Please let Sara know how much she meant to me, and how much joy she brought to my life. Oh how I wish I could be there for her——the day she marries; watching you walk her down the aisle, growing old and wrinkly with you, bouncing our grand babies on our laps. It breaks my heart to know we won't share those memories together. I've seen the pain I've put you through being sick, and now you're finding out about Sara. I'm so sorry, my love, so sorry. I'll love you always Joey, always. I hope that someday you can find it in your heart to forgive me.

Loving you from Heaven, Your Wife Brooke

Tears rolled down my cheeks as I folded the letter. I didn't wipe them away; it felt good to let them run down my face. It felt as though they were washing away all the anger, pain, and hurt feelings from the last few days. I whispered, "It was never your fault Brooke, never. There is nothing to forgive beautiful. I miss you so much, so much sometimes I find it hard to breathe." I was so caught up in the letter and telling

Brooke how much I missed her, that I didn't notice the butterflies that were flying around me. I stood up and looked around the cemetery. What I saw was majestic; the entire cemetery was engulfed with butterflies. Everyone in the cemetery stood motionless and watched in amazement.

CHAPTER 11

Butterflies

Four Years Later...

"Pumpkin, are you ready?"

"Yes, Daddy. I'm just grabbing Mommy's book. I'm coming, I'm coming." I smiled listening to Sara's tiny feet pitter-patter down the hall. I looked down at my daughter, who was holding Brooke's Bible under her arm with her monkey dangling from her other hand. Ever since I told Sara that the Bible on the nightstand was Brooke's, it's been her favorite book. She has me read it to her every night and she takes it everywhere we go.

I knelt down beside her, looked into those dazzling green eyes, and asked, "Are you sure you want to take Mommy's book? You're going to get tired of carrying it around."

"No daddy, I won't."

"Okay," I smiled and pulled down her pink polka-dotted dress. Her sandy blonde hair was combed into two cute pig tales. Thank God for Izzy; every time I combed Sara's hair, it was a mess. The horn from Izzy's car was our cue that it was time to go. I scooped Sara up into my arms and ran out the door.

Izzy smiled at us as we came out of the house. Sara was extremely excited to see Billy.

"Daddy, Daddy! Are we picking up Uncle Billy?"

"Yes Pumpkin." She giggled as I strapped her in the back seat and tickled her belly. We built Billy a room at our warehouse. He helped with cleaning and organizing and would even help Carroll with the books; he was a huge help. But, he wouldn't accept any money. As he put it, he 'doesn't ever want to be dependent on money again'. He was happy with a room, a place to wash up, and a warm cup of coffee. I smiled as I thought about Billy. He and Phil got along just fine, which I was glad about. Although, they did get into the occasional argument about football: Phil's team the Seattle Seahawks, and Billy's native team, the New Orleans Saints.

I hopped in the front seat, looked at Izzy and said, "Ready to rock Doc."

She grimaced, "You and that 'Doc' phrase, seriously Joe." I laughed out loud.

"Sorry Izzy." She wasn't too crazy about Izzy either, but I felt Isabella was too long, and I definitely wasn't going to call her Bella. After Sara went into remission, Dr. Rossi took over her care. We would see her every month for Sara's checkup. We both knew there was something there, but it was too soon for me. It wasn't until about a year ago that I finally asked her to come over for dinner with Sara and I. We'd been seeing each other ever since. We were taking it slow, but it helped that she was crazy about Sara.

Billy was waiting outside when we drove up. He hopped in the back seat saying 'hello' to Izzy and I, then gave all of his attention to Sara. "Hey munchkin, how you doing today?" Sara giggled.

"I'm not a munchkin!"

Billy began tickling her saying, "Oh yes you are." Sara asked Billy if he was excited about going to see the butterflies. "Oh yes I am, I'm always excited about seeing one of God's miracles." I thought about the word Billy chose, *miracle*. Was it a miracle? I mean, there were scientists who had already come up with a theory about the caterpillars migrating to the cemetery. They said that this specific breed of caterpillar had been known to migrate in mass colonies, but they still hadn't been able to explain why every year, on the same day and time, the cocoons hatched into butterflies. Now, people from every corner of the world show up to watch this spectacular event.

I pondered about the events that took place the day Sara was saved. The way Phil found me at the professor's that day. Could that be explained as luck? I doubt it. And showing up before Rasmussen could hurt the girl on the couch, was it all meant to be? Did God put us in all the right places at the right time? It turned out that Professor Rasmussen had been committing that heinous act on a number female aides or students at the college for years. Five more women came forward once Rasmussen was caught. They all made the same statement; they weren't sure that anyone would believe them because of his stature at the college and the way he planned it all out. Then, there was Harry and Rose; they weren't supposed to be here in Seattle and yet, other circumstances kept them here. I felt a touch of sadness as I remembered Harry the day he lost his Rose. I never got a chance to thank Harry. His grandson called me the following day, telling me Harry had died in his sleep that night. I guess Harry couldn't go a day without his Rose. I smiled, picturing Harry's proud look as he took Rose's arm in his that day on the ferry.

When we arrived at the cemetery, it was a circus. There were news cameras and photographers everywhere. The signs saying: 'Lepidopterology Study in Progress, now made sense. It meant 'scientists who study butterflies'. We got out of the car looking around the sea of faces for Rich and Carroll; she said they were already here waiting for us. I talked to Phil this morning and he was fishing with a few of his buddies up in Alaska. He told me to tell everyone 'hi' and to give a kiss to Brooke's headstone for him. We had to park on the other side of the cemetery today because of all the cars, vans, and news crews; so did Carroll. This was the first time we had parked this far from Brooke's grave. Every year that the caterpillars showed up, it became more wide spread throughout the media. They called it, 'The Miracle in Seattle'. This just meant less and less parking in the cemetery, making more room for all the visitors.

We finally found Carroll in the crowd. The first thing she said when she saw us was, "My God, it's a circus here! It's worse than last year."

"It sure is." I agreed, laughing.

Rich just smiled, grabbed her hand, and said, "I'll guide you through the crowd, my dear." Carroll laughed.

"Oh my knight in shining armor." We all laughed and headed towards Brooke's grave. I was carrying Sara as we walked through the sea of people, when I noticed a man with his little girl on his shoulders. I smiled seeing the little girl's excitement and the man's face beaming with pride. Seeing this made me think, *who I would be without Sara?* I shuttered at the thought. But it was true; Brooke was right about me not being able to get her pregnant. I had a conversation with Izzy. She scheduled me an appointment with a fertility specialist. It turns out that I suffer from Azoospermia, which prevents me from being able to have children. I bounced Sara up and down as she laughed and giggled saying, "Higher daddy." I was a happy man; God gave me Sara, and I couldn't have asked for more. Looking at all the people here today, who came to watch the butterflies, made me wonder, *why here?* And why on the same day that I came to read Brooke's letter four years ago. As these thoughts crossed my mind, I heard someone calling my name.

"Joe, Joe Connelly? Joe, hey Joe." I stopped and looked around at the crowd.

Sara asked, "Why did you stop Daddy?"

"I could have sworn someone was calling me, Pumpkin." Sara also started to look around. Then, I saw this lady coming toward me through the crowd, waving her hand and smiling at me. When she got closer, I recognized her right away. It was Joanne, Jimmy's mom. She managed to get through the crowd and was now in front of me.

"Hi Mrs. Anderson, how are you?"

She smiled and said, "Fine, but please call me Joanne."

I replied, "Oh sorry, Joanne." I looked around, "Where's Jim?"

"This must be Sara!" She said avoiding the question. "Oh my God, she's the spitting image of Brooke."

Sara looked at me as she whispered, "Who is this lady Daddy?"

"Now Sara, where are your manners? Say hi to Joanne."

Sara put out her hand, and said, "Nice to meet you. My name is Sara."

Joanne smiled, enclosed her hand around Sara's tiny hand, and said, "Hello Sara. I'm Joanne, it's so nice to meet you."

"How do you know my Daddy?"

"Sara, Pumpkin, why all of the questions?"

"We knew each other a few years ago, when I met your mommy in the hospital," Joanne answered. Sara lit up.

"You knew my Mommy?"

"Yes, and you know what?"

"What?" Sara asked anxiously.

"You look just like her!"

"My daddy says that all the time," Sara replied smiling. My arm grew tired from holding Sara, so I put her down and held her hand.

Izzy came up from behind and said, "I thought you disappeared on me. I turned around and you were nowhere to be found." Izzy looked at Joanne and smiled as I made the introductions.

"Joanne this is Izzy," she gave me a look as I corrected myself smiling at her, "I mean Isabella." They shook hands. "This is Jimmy's mom."

Izzy's eyes widened as she said, "Oh, I'm sorry Joanne. Joe told me so much about Jimmy. How great of a kid he was and well..."

"Thanks, but its fine. I know where he is, and that makes me happy."

"Yes, I'm sure it does," Izzy said and took Sara's hand. "I'll be right over here Joe." I thanked her as she stepped away with Sara, giving Joanne and I some space.

"So where's Jim?" I asked again. She looked at me with sad eyes.

"Well, Joe, he took Jimmy's passing pretty hard. We both did. He went back to work trying to work away his pain. Then, I got involved with church. And, well, we would argue about the most meaningless things. We just couldn't find a way back after losing Jimmy, and he hated how involved I got with church—having Bible studies at our home, even after the butterflies. He just refused to believe and buried himself in his work. We both realized it wasn't going to work. He left me the house and we divorced. He calls every now and then when he comes to the cemetery to see Jimmy, but he never comes on his birthday."

I was thrown by this news about Jim and Joanne's divorce; they seemed to be made for each other. "So Jimmy's here, at this cemetery?" She laughed out loud.

"Well of course Joe. Why do you think all of these people are here?" I looked at her confused. "You're serious, you don't know?" I stared at Joanne and began worrying about her sanity—maybe the loss of Jimmy was too much and she lost touch with reality. Joanne saw the way I was looking at her and she said, "Joe, I'm not crazy, if that's what you're thinking. You're the one who put this in Jimmy's head… about our bodies being cocoons and our souls being butterflies flying up to Heaven to be with Jesus." I looked at her for a moment, then I remembered the story my dad told me about Uncle Carl.

"Jimmy told you the story?"

"Yes he did, and about how he wasn't afraid of dying because Jesus was coming for him, so he asked me not to be sad when he dies. He told me, 'I'm a butterfly Mom. I'll be in Heaven with God and his son Jesus." Joanne's eyes filled with tears at this memory. I was blown away by what she was telling me.

"So, you think this butterfly phenomenon has something to do with Jimmy?" Joanne smiled knowingly at me.

"What is today's date?" I still wasn't understanding her question.

"Um, well it's July fourteenth."

"Today is Jimmy's birthday." I looked at her stunned; I mean, that was a huge coincidence. I was in disbelief. Joanne smiled at my reaction. "There's something else…" I stared at her, still trying to register the information.

"What?"

"What time, every year on the same day, do the butterflies start leaving the cocoons?"

"Well they've calculated it to be roughly around one forty-two in the afternoon."

Joanne then reached in her purse and pulled out a piece of paper that resembled a city document. She handed it to me, and when I realized what it was, I thought, *no, there's no way.* I mean, but it was plain as day written here before me; it was Jimmy's birth certificate and it stated that he was born on July fourteenth at one forty-two pm. The exact same time that the butterflies leave their cocoons every year.

I felt my knees go weak all of the sudden. I felt a warm feeling run through my body as if I was touched by something warm. All the hairs on my arms were standing up like I had been shocked by electricity. Then, tears began running down my face as I was hit with knowing, really knowing; I felt it run throughout my entire body. Joanne hugged me as she shed tears of her own. I hugged her back; it was a connection, a feeling that could not be denied. I slowly let go of Joanne and gave her back Jimmy's birth certificate, wiping the tears from my eyes. She smiled and said, "It's beautiful isn't it?" I looked around still choking back tears.

"Yes, yes, it is."

"I have to meet with my church at Jimmy's grave."

"Alright. It was nice seeing you Joanne." She turned to walk away. "Joanne…" she turned back to face me. "Thank you." She understood what I meant.

She walked up to me, took my hand in hers and said, "No Joe, thank you; for Brooke giving my Jimmy his faith and helping me find mine." She touched my cheek then turned and walked away, disappearing into the sea of people waiting to see the butterflies.

I walked over to find Izzy and Sara. "Come on, let's get to Mommy's grave before the butterflies come out." I scooped Sara into my arms as we hurried to Brooke's grave.

Sara looked at my face and asked, "Daddy, have you been crying?"

"Maybe just a little Pumpkin," I smiled.

"Why Daddy?"

"Well, Pumpkin, I just heard some really good news." When we got to Brooke's grave, Billy, Carroll, and Rich were there smiling at us as we walked up.

Carroll looked at her watch, "It's almost time Joey." I smiled at Carroll, walked over to Brooke's headstone, and was taken aback by what I saw. Brookes headstone was covered in cocoons. Hardly an inch of the stone could be seen except for a perfect heart that left the words 'Beloved wife and mother' uncovered. I heard Carroll's gasp as she noticed it too. She could only utter a barely audible, "Oh my God." Sara walked over to Brooke's headstone.

"Look Daddy, look! It's a heart. The butterflies love Mommy." I smiled at Sara and picked her up.

"That's your Mommy's way of letting us know she loves us too and she's always here watching over us." Izzy looked over at me and Sara with tears in her eyes as she touched my shoulder. Billy knelt beside Brooke's grave with his head bowed and prayed. I could hear him thanking God for letting us know he has not forgotten about his children. I put Sara down and she sat next to Billy. My dad's story about the cocoons and the butterflies came to mind. I pictured Jimmy's freckled face smiling while he told Jesus the story. It always baffled me that Brooke passed away on the same day as Jimmy. She did mention her mother and Jimmy right before she passed. A tear slid down my cheek as these thoughts ran through my mind.

I looked around at all the people waiting in excitement for the cocoons to hatch. I had questioned over the years if it was a miracle or just migrating caterpillars. Looking around at the sea of people— young, old, black, white, brown, yellow—it didn't matter who they were. They all stood waiting to see a miracle. As I stood, taking it all in, I realized that the true miracle is us—God's children all standing here together. The cocoons turning into butterflies before our eyes was just a metaphor; God was letting us know that it doesn't end here. These graves hold the bodies of our loved ones, but not their souls.

All I could do was smile and think of my beautiful wife. She was right. She knew the truth. That's why she never doubted nor questioned God. Even as she endured tremendous struggle, her faith never wavered. I turned my eyes to the sky and prayed, "I'm sorry God, I'm sorry that I doubted you. You were right Brooke, and boy was I wrong. I guess God had to wink at me to get my attention. My faith will never waiver again, my love."

Just then, the butterflies began leaving their cocoons. I watched as Sara jumped up and down screaming with joy, "Look Daddy, look." The entire cemetery went silent as the butterflies left their cocoons; there were thousands upon thousands of them. In the deafening silence of the crowd, you could hear the sound of the butterflies' wings as they carried the whispers of our loved ones, the words of God, and a promise that's been unbreakable since the beginning of time. Sara ran up to me and jumped into my arms.

"I love you Daddy."

"I love you too Pumpkin."

"How much?" I knew what she meant. I put two fingers on her chin and she did the same to me; we both smiled. Then, she asked me something that surprised me.

"Who's Jimmy Daddy? I looked at her shocked.

"How do you know that name?"

"I heard the lady, Joanne, say his name."

"Jimmy…" I paused as I looked around. All the people stood mesmerized by the butterflies as they fluttered around the cemetery. "Jimmy's the man," I told her. Sara ran off, twirling as the butterflies danced around her, singing. "Jimmy's the man, Jimmy's the man!" I stood up, looked toward the sky again, and said, "You Jimmy, you the man."

The End

www.ingramcontent.com/pod-product-compliance
Lightning Source LLC
Chambersburg PA
CBHW020047180626
46812CB00006B/2223